T0341457

Settlers of Unassigned Lands

Settlers of Unassigned Lands

Stories

Charles McLeod

University of Michigan Press
Ann Arbor

Published in the United States of America by the
University of Michigan Press

Printed and bound by CPI Group (UK) Ltd, Croydon, CR0 4YY

2018   2017   2016   2015   4   3   2   1

DOI: http://dx.doi.org/10.3998/tfcp.13240728.0001.001

ISBN 978-0-472-11955-4 (hardcover : alk. paper)
ISBN 978-0-472-03620-2 (paper : alk. paper)
ISBN 978-0-472-12103-8 (e-book)

Contents

Acknowledgments

Stories in this collection appeared in the following publications: "How to Start Your Own Midwestern Ghost Town" in *Third Coast* and on *Joyland*; "Exit Wounds" in *ZYZZYVA*; "Settlers of Unassigned Lands" in *South Dakota Review*; "The Ledge" in *CutBank*; "Rancho Brava" on *Web Conjunctions*. The author wishes to extend his thanks to these publications and their editors for their permission to publish the stories in this collection.

Thank you to my family; my friends; the University of Virginia MFA Program; the Fine Arts Work Center in Provincetown; Martha Heasley Cox and the Center for Steinbeck Studies at San Jose State University; Jen Hancock; TJ Gerlach; Colorado Mesa University; Aaron McCollough; Matthew Vollmer; and Kelsey Yoder.

How to Start Your Own Midwestern Ghost Town

First, locate a town in the upper portion of the Central Time Zone. Population circa 1990 should hover around five hundred. Median income should be not enough. Next, make sure industry leaves: the meat plant, the Wheat Growers, the regional K-Mart equivalent—all of these must go. Try to space the closings out over a decade or more; the effect you are after is chronic fatigue, as opposed to acute calamity. Make the pace of the obliteration glacial. Think, slow burn. The Midwest is filled with distance and if you are going to start your own ghost town, it's important to realize it won't happen overnight. Let the chain stores crunch their numbers. Watch them downsize, have sales, take losses, give up. See local business follow suit: The Hamburger Shack, the Tractor and Auto, the church thrift shop with its copper, polished bell above the door. It will be mandatory, too, to have your town's high school incorporated into another's; youth are often on the receiving end of mixed messages, but busing them twenty or forty or sixty miles five days a week will make certain they understand it foolish to settle where they were raised, that their town is dying, that even education has left.

Subsidize all the farms. Subsidize everyone. If they own pets, subsidize those. Keep the machines out of the fields. Promote sloth. Give people time to dwell, to ponder, to watch six hours of Court TV each evening, the satellite dish turned skyward like the face of Job. Make sure the governor cuts hospital funds so it takes over an hour for an ambulance to reach you, ensuring if a serious accident does occur you will expire while waiting for help. At seven o'clock on a Thursday, come home from work and have your wife hand you divorce papers. She's gone three towns over for these, the courthouse in your small burg long dissolved, its rooms of law gutted, the flagpoles and desk lamps and stenography machine donated to the failing church thrift shop. Watch your wife leave in her brother's pickup. Open a beer. Open more.

The next day drive to the gas station hungover. Here is where you bought your first candy bar, first cigarettes, first three-pack of lubricated condoms. Stare at the man dismantling the pumps. Stare at the gas station across the street, closed now for over a year, the windows boarded, tumbleweeds—real tumbleweeds—wedged behind the empty pop machine. Get out of your truck. Throw up.

Arrive to your clerking job at the courthouse three towns over, where your wife obtained her divorce papers yesterday. Sit on your chair behind bulletproof glass, listening to people who can't pay their court fees tell you why they can't pay their court fees. Let them ramble. Suggest a payment plan. Never smile; it will be taken as a symbol of aggression. Elderly women may claw at the window if you do this. High school football stars, now middle-aged drunks, may head butt the glass you sit behind then try the electronically locked door to your left (their right). Stay calm. Listen to the door rattle. Call security. Go to lunch.

Watch your friends come in, your neighbors. Talk about caulking the bathtub or grouting kitchen tile, talk about anything more pleasant than the task at hand. See them slide their papers over the recessed iron receptacle. Pretend to not notice their fingers shaking. Look elsewhere while they count out bags of change. Block out phrases like "tax liens" and "loan payments" and "farm repossession." When they ask you if you can hold off on running the check until the end of the week, tell them that you'll see what you can do. What you can do is exactly nothing. Depress your PAYMENT RECEIVED stamp against its red felt blotter. Consider that humanity is drowning in its own bureaucracy, that it creates more problems than it solves. Use your stamp on all three copies. Forget the last place to get gasoline in your town has closed forever. Make it home on fumes.

Saturday afternoon attend the Veterans' Parade. See the men who served ride grim-faced in the back seats of near mint, old model convertibles, their hands raised gamely to the crowd. Wonder who can afford to keep these cars, and for how much longer. Scald your tongue on coffee from your thermos. Ogle the teenage baton twirler at the motorcade's head. Think about the boy she'll meet at college, her future home in a suburb of Chicago or Milwaukee. Realize this is what she has been thinking about every night for the past two years, her ACT now taken, her applications in the mail, the processing fees exhausting the tip money from her summer work at the Tastee-Freez, the same one your wife punched in at so long ago. Realize that come spring this girl will check the mailbox daily, praying, really praying, that God might grant her leave from a township now surviving on teen pregnancy and checks from the Feds. See her toss and catch, toss and catch. Enjoy the high cut of her sequined leotard. Remember the state census is due out in a week's time. Watch the brightly colored parade balloons float up, and away.

At home, decide to go birding. This will involve emptying half of your thermos of the coffee you took to the parade and replacing it with Kentucky grain alcohol. It is important also to bring binoculars, not so much for viewing the birds as to justify, should someone happen upon you, why you might be seated in the patch of woods by the sewage treatment plant, shit-canned and mumbling to yourself. Regard the plumage of a blue jay as you zip through your toddy. Stagger upright and urinate on an elm. For as long as you can linger in the small glen, because now there is nothing waiting at home for you but leftovers and nighttime television and then Sunday morning, when it feels simply cruel to find yourself alone.

Around midnight, call your wife at her brother's house. Plead epiphany. Beg for another chance. Admit you made a big mistake but that it was not done with conscious irresponsibility, that it was a situation that was unforeseeable, that by the time you knew what was happening, the outcome could not be changed. Past your wife's angry breathing hear the Union Pacific blow its whistle as it passes through on the tracks. Remember the Cabela's gift card you got for your brother-in-law last Christmas. Consider the make of the rifle he'd chosen. Hang up. Lock the doors. Pass out.

The morning of the Lord's Day burn eggs in a pan on the stovetop then rummage around in your basement while drinking more beer. Find old yearbooks and ancient Christmas cards, moth-eaten wrestling tights and your dead father's collection of suits. Find shoeboxes labeled SPARK PLUGS and FLY LURES and BAKELITE. Find trophies that seem barely your own. Go upstairs and call the county courthouse, leaving a message on your supervisor's voicemail saying that you won't be in tomorrow. Make a day of your self-pity and remorse. Use the start of the workweek to recover. Feel good about your decision. Feel like this is something you've earned. Go back downstairs and thumb through a wooden crate of license plates, souvenirs taken from cars left to rust in the county impound lot, the owners unable or not wanting to get them out. Put on trucker's hats and work shirts and long aprons bearing the name and logo of defunct companies running from the Rust Belt to the Great Plains: Bethlehem Steel, Hemingray Glass, the Manitowoc Shipbuilding Company; Midway Airlines, Hafner Manufacturing, Wyoming Heating and Oil. If you're feeling brave, peruse old photo albums of you and your wife on your wedding day, on your honeymoon, standing in front of your financed two-bedroom house. Ignore the single piece of furniture that resides here, a white sheet drawn over its top.

Before the sun fades and night falls, write down the names of all the people you've known who have departed your town in the past decades: childhood friends and generations of families, mayors and teachers and priests. Wear your pencil's sharp tip to a nub. Realize that if the numbers really are accurate, your town has lost around two hundred people, forty percent of its total population, since the five-hundred mark of 1990. Wonder if the larger world is even aware of this. Wonder if anyone cares at all.

On your personal holiday drive to the county library two towns south, stopping for gas at the first place that has it. Buy a six-pack for later. Buy five key chains you'll never use. Do this out of shame for still having a job when so many are jobless, for getting paychecks from the state drawn on the backs of the unlucky, the speeders, the driving drunks. Realize the cashier behind the counter is one of these people, that she orally hurled saliva at you just last week, while you explained in the flat tone of an automated voice prompt why the court-processing fee was more than her gas bill. Recall the woman's daughter dressed in pastel rags, her blonde curls a dirty mat, her toes poking through the tops of her black canvas shoes. Picture the spittle hitting the bulletproof glass. When the cashier asks, while glaring at you, what you want with so many key chains, say you're doing some early Christmas shopping. Don't tell her this is your way of trying to stimulate the economy. Don't tell her this is your way of trying to help.

At the library's circulation desk put your name down on the waiting list to use the only computer. A good measure of whether or not your future ghost town will garner success is the amount of income the people in your area can spend on home technology. Look at the number thirty-seven next to your signature on the list.

While you are waiting wander over to the shelves that house the history section. Finger the spines of titles concerning the Mayans and Spaniards, the Inca and smallpox, the Goths' and Gauls' and Teutons' descent upon Rome.

Gaze at the surplus of writing on ancient civilizations and the details of how they failed. Think *The Grapes of Wrath* has been shelved incorrectly. Realize that it has not. Turn the row's corner and find yourself in the parenting section, surrounded by books on fertilization and birthing technique, breathing method and back labor, diet while pregnant and aerobics while pregnant and final trimester care. *Baby names and their etymological meanings. God's intent for your newborn. Foundations for raising a capable child.* Grow anxious. Feel your hands go clammy. Find a side exit and get to your truck. Put down two bottles from the six-pack you bought earlier. Watch a turkey vulture ride the noon vapors above.

After forty-five more minutes of waiting, sit down on the still-warm plastic seat facing the computer screen. Enter the address of the major Internet auction site. From your jeans pocket remove the piece of paper with the details of the item (Wooden Baby's Crib, Barely Used) you're looking to sell. Post your listing while the man in line behind you looks over your shoulder. Lend him a stare that lets him know if he doesn't locate some patience, you can meet him in the parking lot and provide him with some of your own. Enter all information needed by the auction site on your third try. Go out to your vehicle and drive home.

In your kitchen, dump the contents of your peppershaker out on the counter. Ignore the garbage can, its plume of refuse. Ignore the pots rotting through in the sink. Bend down to the counter's top and put a few lines of pepper up either nostril. Call the courthouse to say your illness is worse than you initially figured, that it looks like the full week will have to be spent at home. Cough up phlegm dotted with black flecks while talking. Understand you've stooped to a new low.

At sunset go back to the woods by the sewage treatment plant, a fresh thermos of coffee and bourbon tucked under your arm in the manner a small child holds a favorite toy. Forget to bring your set of binoculars. Sit amongst the leaves and nettles in the crisp November air. Watch the light slant golden through limbs of thinning foliage, the beams seemingly still but having actually traveled faster than you can calculate, from the cold void of space to your makeshift forest of gloom. Find your favorite elm and relieve yourself just as a couple who live down the street from you come over the wood's small hill. Wave with your free hand, slurring your words as you try to explain yourself. Prepare for another long night at home.

Tuesday morning wake early for work, forcing yourself to revitalize, vowing inner strength and investment in the future, vowing never to have a string of days like you just had again. Clean some dishes. Make some coffee. Remove the bulbous heap of refuse to the can around the side of the house. On your way back in, stop to pick up your state capital's daily newspaper from your doorstep. The census numbers will have made the front page. Don't begin to weep internally. Don't throw up in your mouth. It is important to think of this enormous, damning, confirming article as free publicity for your future ghost town, and not the death of everything you know and love. Find your county in the third line of the cover story, listed as the prime example of rural decay. Read quotes from your governor positing why people are treating your region as though it were plague-ridden. Stare at the picture of him in a suit. Stare at the three-color bar graphs and pie charts, replete with statistics on education and income, home values and unemployment rates, marital status and births versus deaths. Hear your phone ring from inside the house.

Lose your job. In the manner standard to Midwestern nicety, engage in a fifteen-minute conversation with your supervisor about bass season and Big Ten football, maintaining an upbeat tone while you wait for him to can you. Flip through the paper's classifieds section while your now ex-boss lists off the necessary euphemisms, words that hurtle through your county like the steel-tracked freight trains do, unstoppable, not slowing: cutbacks, deficits, closures, defeat. Wonder what your new life in the big city will be like. Wonder how much you can get for your house. Wonder if you aren't smarter than the criminals on Court TV who burn their houses for the insurance money. Think *you* might be able to not leave behind clues. Write down your severance pay with the same pencil you used to make your RECENTLY DEPARTED list. Hang up the phone. Convert the severance figure to a living wage. Go outside and get the birds off the trees with your screams. Look down the length of your short quaint street where small good things were supposed to happen for you, a place where you could manage through the seasons with a weathered, stoic sort of dignity, assured that you will not conquer the world but also that the world will not conquer you. See not one other human soul.

Drive to the grocery store for more beer. Over the store's front window regard the poorly draped banner, its red block letters reading FINAL WEEK. Wonder if the masses of medieval Europe felt like this during the waves of Black Death, the disaster in real time, fully spelled out. Watch people buy everything they can in a panic, a last gasp, the carts of the elderly filled to capacity, mothers too young to purchase a six pack of Grain Belt buying Pampers en masse. Think the crowd should be much larger than it is. Realize it actually should not, that the size is just right, that according to the census your town has lost 54% of its population in fifteen years—unthinkable, impossible, correct.

Near the row of gumball machines next to the sliding doors get cornered by an out-of-town reporter. Answer her questions about your region's exodus in a manic fashion reserved most often for the mentally ill. When she asks if you have children tell her you used to. When she asks you if you're married tell her not anymore. Pull a cart from its column as she says thank you. Walk the worn linoleum aisles. Remember coming here with your father after Sunday school and filling white bags of waxed paper with candy, the clear plastic scoops on their ropes. Remember stealing a six pack after a wrestling match on a Saturday night, your pickup, much newer then, idling in the parking lot, your future wife in the front seat, having told you just minutes ago that if you put a ring on her finger she won't bother with college applications, that all she needs to be happy for the rest of her life is you. Remember coming here three years ago, minutes before midnight, just beating the doors being locked for the evening, and informing the teenage clerk that your wife is pregnant and at home, and if you don't come back with two pints of mint chip ice cream and a half dozen peppered jerky sticks it may be better if you don't come back at all. Turn a corner and see a sign taped to the glass door of the freezer that holds bags of ice, reading: NOTH-ING LEFT HERE. Take the sign down. Add it to your cart.

After checkout, on your way past the gumball machines, catch part of a conversation between two of the men who rode in the Veterans' Parade. Look at their wooden canes and weathered denims and pressed gingham shirts. Notice they are joking, laughing, that this is somehow not the apocalypse to them but part of the continuum of life. Just as you are leaving, just as the door is shutting, just as you are mentally committing to your new existence in your state's capital, hear it come from one of the men's mouths, the words that will make all the difference, the single sentence that you have been unknowingly waiting for these weeks and months and years. Hear the grizzled veteran say: "This place is a god damned ghost town—you'd think someone could at least capitalize on *that.*"

For the first time in so long see with absolute clarity. Realize your path. Know its way. Tell the man that he is exactly god damned right while you wheel your cart out the door, stuffing all four twelve packs into the donation bin for the county food drive. You do not need them anymore. You are lucid. You are able. You are wise beyond your years.

There is a ghost town to start, and it is time to set to work.

Begin by cataloguing all items in your basement: the fly lures, the bakelite, the spark plugs, the license plates; the long aprons and work shirts and state wrestling trophies and suits. Anything a collector might consider antique. Anything someone will pay good money for to not use. When you are finished with your list run to the home of an elderly neighbor, demanding that she let you borrow the digital camera her grandkids in Denver gave her last Christmas, your aggressive manner of asking assuring she can't say no. Return to your basement and begin snapping pictures. Remove the white sheet from the crib you've kept stored here for over a year now, taking pictures of it for good measure, though under the rules of your new ghost town you will no longer sell this item. Under the rules of your new ghost town it will now function as a centerpiece or cornerstone, a symbol for what has been and is yet to come.

Drive to the library, passing by the elderly neighbor's house while she stares at you from behind her screen door. Do a sort of thing with your hand that is meant to imply: *you can trust me! I'll be right back!* Among the columns and rows of books find the librarian and force her to show you how to plug the camera into the single computer. When she tells you that the cords that came with the camera are needed to do that, tell her she better find some, and fast. See her respond to your threat, locating the accessories you need from a locked filing cabinet next to the water fountain. Take the clipboard housing the wait list for the computer off the counter of the circulation desk and begin calling out names. When someone responds, wave your checkbook in their face, saying, *I will pay you twenty dollars to move ahead of you in line. This is not a joke. I am going to save my hometown starting right now. The check is good. Yes or no?* Do this twenty-three times. Write twenty-three checks. Sit down on your earned throne and click the icon that gets you online.

Remove the list of basement findings from your jeans pocket. Delete your old posting and add one hundred and fifty-two new ones. Receive help in wording the descriptions of your items from your high school English teacher, a plump woman with a weakness for romance novels who has been on unemployment since your alma mater was shut down. Have her pat you on the head, tell you what a good thing you're doing. Realize this is the first human contact you've had since your wife left you for good. Log off and return the cords to the librarian, her anger replaced by fascination. Listen to her ask if there's anything else she can do. Tell her you need the names of enormous Midwestern philanthropic foundations, the kind that treat money the way people at weddings treat rice. Discover someone has put together a book of these groups. Flip through the hundred-plus listings, scrawling down information on squares of library scratch paper with your borrowed, miniature pencil. On a separate sheet, compose your letter. Write something similar to this:

Dear Sons and Daughters of Benevolent Millionaires,

Perhaps you're aware of the recent census numbers for my city, county, and state. They are not good. Everyone has left or is leaving; there are no jobs, and we are running out of places to buy food. What I am proposing is to not combat these truths but rather absorb them and prosper thusly, to accept the fate the rest of the country has consigned to us and try to keep all remaining inhabitants here alive. In short, I want to save the place I live from turning into a ghost town by turning it into one. I would appreciate greatly your support. I am planning whole blocks of gift shops and ghost town attractions, a food court and animal rides for the kids. What I need most badly is capital to get started. This is where you come in. Without your help everyone here is completely doomed. Winter is coming. I await your response.

Sincerely,

The Name You Have Had Since Birth

Using the librarian's personal laptop computer, download and print out and fill out application form after application form with the determination of the teenage baton twirler from the Veterans' Parade. Understand her urgency now, her drive. Think your wife must have had this same drive in her while handing out chocolate malts and chili fries and bacon burgers at the Tastee-Freez all those years ago, college only months away until she started dating you. When you are finished with your forms, make seventeen photocopies of your letter. Go to the post office and buy seventeen stamps. Kiss each envelope before dropping it into the mailbox, these pieces of paper your livelihood now, the very rest of your life.

Drive home. Draw the blinds. Find your pencil. Begin work on coupons and maps and brochures for tourists arriving to your very impending ghost town. Sketch hay rides, a corn maze, The Virtual Tornado Chaser. Sketch figures panning for fool's gold in your manmade stream. Lure and capture the all-white tabby you often glimpse wandering by the defunct train depot, the building so haunted-seeming high schoolers won't go there to use drugs. Add your own likeness to your drawing, walking the tabby on a Day-Glo leash. Create The Abandoned Farm Restaurant, The Lost Thread Quilt Shop, Thee Olde Tyme Dust Bowl Saloon. Keep at it. Don't give up. Remember other towns in the area are vying to become ghost towns also, and someone out there may be working just as hard as you. Design parking lots and information kiosks. Design a combination petting barn and German buffet. Design The Safety Gourd, a small building for children who have become separated from their parents, a designated "safe place" painted bright orange and in the shape of an acorn squash. Never consider this a mockery of the heartland, a joke you've played on yourself and those around you. Justify your plan as progressive thinking, that what the Midwest can offer is changing and that you are bringing the tourist industry, a growth industry, to its door.

Midweek take to your truck, scouting your town and those towns around you for notices of upcoming yard sales and farm auctions. Cruise the streets at five miles an hour, scanning the rows of houses the way vengeful gang members do in films. When attending one of these events purchase anything that functions as a remnant of times passed, that recalls the ethic and industry and independence on which your part of the country once prided itself. Fill the bed of your pickup with crates and boxes. Haggle, barter, hoodwink, persist. Catch the last of the autumn flea markets, the days growing noticeably shorter, the sort of cold in the air that makes your lungs start upon initial breath of it, the mallard and geese and teal gone south. Behind card tables see your brethren seated in folding chairs, bundled in blankets, wondering if they too should migrate somewhere else. Buy what they sell for tough but fair prices. In your mind promise all of them brand new ghost town jobs, even your ex-wife and her brother, even the gas station store clerk who spat at you. Return to the library. Open your inbox. Look at the dozens of bids for items you've auctioned. Answer questions about shipping to Japan and Australia. Respond by saying you will send your waking nightmare to anywhere in the world.

Tonight, in your empty bed, come up with ideas for highway signs for your ghost town, huge advertisements that will sit just off the blacktop and indicate you are alive, are here. For a theme, use something extinct or fossilized: cavemen, dinosaurs, petrified wood. Petrified dinosaurs. Something gone but mighty. Something dead but built to last. When the time comes, you will let the banner drop. You will send up the balloons. People will push strollers down the sidewalks again. Hotels, once built, will fill. Let your mind's eye sweep over all you've created. Fall asleep dreaming of what you can do.

Have Thanksgiving pass unnoticed. On the first day of December receive snow. For the last time this year return to the woods by the sewage treatment plant, because your one-year old son seemed to love this place most in winter, the whiteness or quiet of it, the ice-hided boughs. Remember the warmth and weight of his body, snug in its harness, as you carried him on your back. Remember his breath and fingers and murmurs. Remember his last evening on earth, his body seizing in the bathtub, undiagnosed epilepsy, and you away from him for thirty seconds or surely no more than a minute because the phone rang, because the National Census Bureau chose that moment of all moments in your life to phone and remind you to fill out your household's information form, and that by the time you hung up and returned to the bathroom, your child was blue. Remember the sirens, so far in the distance. Remember your sad attempts at CPR. Remember awaiting your wife's return from her night class at the regional community college. Try to forget the quizzical look on her face upon noticing the paramedics lingering on the porch. Find no irony in driving to the largest city in your area, a place teeming with life, to buy a child's coffin on an installment plan.

Irony isn't for a person like you. Irony is for accredited professionals from urban centers. Irony is for patrons of your future ghost town.

In the glen's silence listen to your shoes crunch over the new snow. From its perch on a low branch stare at a bird, some small species, a finch or swallow or type you don't know. Walk closer to the tree. Stand below it. See the bird hold its place. Take a single step closer. Have the bird not move. Hold out your hand. Extend a finger. Watch the bird leave its branch and fly towards you. This will be the most amazing moment of your life.

Exit Wounds

I was renting the attic room of an illegal boarding house, a condemned Victorian run by a mistress of the Chief of Police, but there'd been an argument of some sort between these two parties and the place had been raided, and boards had been nailed up over all the windows and doors. I tried to find my car, but I couldn't find it. So I went down to the Mission and 16th BART station to look for my friend Terry, who sold fake drugs there sometimes. Sure enough, there he was.

"I knew you'd be here," I said.

"Where else do I have to go?" Terry answered. He was crouched down, cutting up a bar of soap with a penknife. The curled peels were landing on a page of newspaper he'd spread out over the ground. The hood of Terry's sweatshirt was ripped off on one side and it made it look like he had a short broken cape attached to himself. Schoolchildren were playing in the afternoon shadows, finding ways to wreck their Catholic plaids.

"Can't they just leave us alone?" I was pointing. The air smelled of water and garbage. People ascended the subway's escalator, pretending we weren't even there.

"You could make yourself useful for once," Terry told me. "Why don't you start filling up these balloons?" From his palm he shook out five or six of the little rubber things, but I didn't feel like working.

"What are we going to call them when we're done?" I asked.

"They're one-and-ones—cocaine and heroin, all mashed up."

"But they're soap."

"Now you've got the music going."

"Do you happen to have any real drugs?" I asked.

"I will after I've sold these," Terry said.

In the upstairs of a thrift store I kept putting items in my pockets. I wanted everything, now that I had nowhere for any of it to go. One of those Guardian Angels in their tilted hats got right up next to me and crossed his arms but I just stood there, staring at the metal shelves of goblets and ceramic junk.

"I saw what you were doing," the Angel said.

"It all looks so lonely," I told him. "I'm only trying to help." That morning, the group of we evicted had stood on the tall sidewalk of Texas Avenue, waiting for the cuffs to snap on. There were ten of us in total, or fifteen, and certainly we had never been gathered like this before, blinking in the sun and horribly aware of one another, figuring out who had cigarettes and who did not. The policemen had brought hammers; they were ripping the shutters off the front of the house and turning them sideways over the windows. The mistress was wailing and being led down the steps.

"My truths, my liberties, my livelihood," she pleaded. Mascara had stained her fake silk dress. Some in our group were prying at her fingers—I had thought we were trying to save her, but we were really only after her rings. When the policemen drew their batons we scattered, spreading like pollen over the city. Mission Street was miles long and I'd been over every inch of it, from the Greyhound station at the foot of the Bridge out to Silver Avenue, where most of the shop signs were in Spanish. But I could never remember what stood where, the specific order of things, so I walked the blocks again and again, checking and rechecking, hoping some wide, precious idea might strike me because I could feel myself getting older, the ports closing, the ships pulling up all their ropes.

Past the doorframe of The Audrey I saw Parnell on a stool. He was nursing a port and shirtless, his brown skin shining in the sun. On weekends, for work, Parnell painted over the track marks on his neck with make-up and did ventriloquism at children's parties. His stage name, I think, was Sultan the Wondrous. His dummy's name was Parnell.

The Audrey itself was a long, narrow bar; until the 80s it had shared a wall with a garment factory but that place had caught fire and its insides had melted, and it would never be rebuilt again. Above the Audrey's booths you could see where the plaster had bubbled and pocked from the heat, the flames wanting more and more. It was an easy place to feel brave in, and this of course was what we were after, to be the survivors of some tragedy that could never have possibly affected us, to live on and on telling lies to strangers about having seen the ashes, and tasted the soot.

Parnell, the real one, lent money on occasion. I was terrified of him, which he admired me for. In this way the two of us had built a relationship based around debt.

"Your car got towed and I'm completely broke," he told me. "It was Jenkins that did it, so you know."

"Are you sure you don't have *any* money?" I asked him. The Audrey was empty except for the two of us. Parnell just sat there and shrugged. "I'm drinking on vouchers the bartender made me. You can ask him yourself when he gets back."

"Where did he go in the first place?"

"His dog's dying. He took it to the vet."

"Jenkins hit that ambulance last Saturday on Valencia. His wrecker's all smashed to pieces now. How did the bartender make you those vouchers? No one would believe that, not a species on earth."

"My pockets are empty," Parnell said. "There aren't parties for months."

Over his back were tattoos that spelled out lines from the Scripture; I could make out the *shalls* and the *haths* and the *wants*. From the stool next to him, Parnell lifted up his puppet. Its legs swung on their twined pulleys. The wood face looked just like Parnell's own.

"I could do a show for you," he said, brightening. "I could practice my routine." Parnell stuck his arm into the guts of the dummy. The Audrey's television was on but the sound was off. Around a lawn diamond in a different time zone athletes stood waiting and here I was thinking of them, when they would never, ever think of me. Past the bar's door a bus gasped, accelerating toward somewhere else. For a moment it blocked out the sun entirely and I could see, for the first time, Parnell's eyes. He was flung on dope, just gone.

"You could have saved me some of what you've taken," I told him. "That was a pretty selfish thing to do."

"Help, this man has his hands in me," said the puppet. "Help, help, help, help, help."

"Would you tell if I took a beer from the cooler? Could I get behind there and back out?"

"I don't know, I don't know," said Parnell. "The dog, it was shaking so badly. It was a big thing, a lab or a hound. The people around here, they're just exit wounds. They're just proof that something went wrong."

I leaned over the bar's counter, sliding back the cooler's door. Inside were ice and endless varieties. The columned bottles were sweating, as though it was work just waiting there. There were so many kinds I couldn't make a decision; I started taking all of them out, using my lighter to pry off their tops. The puppet mumbled something about wisdom and courage.

"What did he say?" I asked, finishing one bottle and picking up another.

"Nothing," Parnell said, handing me a voucher. "Don't worry about it at all."

At one point, toward the very end, when my actions had made me a larger monster and there were people, literally, hunting me down, I'd drifted east toward Nevada, though I had somewhere more distant in mind: Cheyenne or Minot or Moline, somewhere so far that if I finally got there, I might not be able to leave. South of Fresno I spent the night at a temple, the monks in their saffron robes. Would you believe me when I say I couldn't speak if I'd wanted to? In the stone room where I spent the night I was completely muted—the silence had been that great. I'd always thought there was a con-nection between misery and religion but there on the nightstand was the Buddha, plump and joyous and wise.

In the morning this silence had lifted, and a younger monk led me to a garden at the center of the temple's confines. Here were rows and rows of tomato plants, their fruit a buoyant red. The two of us knelt down close to the soil.

"You have to brush the aphids off," the monk told me, "but you must do this without killing a single one." In the dawn light he guided my hand over a leaf of a plant, its little hairs like sticky wool.

"I can't see them," I said. "Or it's a trick? They're not really there?"

"It's not a trick," the monk told me.

"I want to be feeling what you're feeling, I promise. But I'm broke and I have miles to go."

"We can give you money, if that's what you're after. Not much, but some, yes."

I tried harder after hearing this. In my mind, though, the usual things came back: shattered glass and the mouths of alleys, sirens and plastic bags. A woman I'd married from fear and abandoned for the same reason. The leaves tore in my fingers, their insides leaking out.

"It would all take so much work to fix," I said.

"It takes the same amount every day," the monk agreed.

It turned out that Parnell did have more of what he'd taken, and in the bathroom of the Audrey I used his needle to dump it into my veins. When I came back out the light had grown loose or aquatic; the shadows from the passing cars wove and swayed like kelp. I'd gone from something crooked and awkward to polished and perfect, round and entirely smooth. I sat down next to Parnell and when I woke up the bartender was yelling at me, his dog there beside him on the ground.

At the top of Dolores Park, one hundred yards above the lanes of grids and streets, a big man who claimed he was a banker asked me for a date. His cowboy boots had silver over their tips and on his right wrist he wore a lady's tennis bracelet, a gold thing with a heart-shaped charm that swung and dangled when he motioned. The steep walk had forced me almost to vomit, but I'd held down my insides and kept my high and now San Francisco was all around me, the lines of houses like rows of teeth. I could see both bridges, the Oakland Hills on the other side of the flat blue bay. The Mission District was broke again; all the people who had made a living from computers had lost their jobs and moved away and the filthy sidewalks belonged once more to us, the addicts and immigrants, the departed and the just-arrived, who were left to hope and rob and wait for the country's next set of good times to roll around, at which point we would again be pushed from sight. It wasn't so bad, either, except for the fact that there were those who told us we were doing something wrong, when we were only doing what they expected.

From the breast pocket of his grey, lined suit the banker brought out a bill. I wasn't nervous; I couldn't feel my face at all.

"I've never done this before," I told him.

"You're going to do it now, though," he said. There were white bits of saliva at the corners of his mouth and he was chewing on a sandwich, the plastic wrap greased and hanging.

"You're from the Midwest, aren't you?" I said. He had the accent and that look to him, too, like he'd been run through with dumb joy. I'd seen it that morning, when I looked in the mirror. I couldn't escape it, though I tried and I tried.

The banker put his hands on my shoulders, pushing downward. "My wife was from Bismarck. Your hair is like hers was. I'm always so hungry. I can't seem to fill up."

I was fumbling with the leather of his belt when a Public Works truck came up the park's winding road, startling the man and sending him away. His money was still in my pocket, though, and I saw him the very next week, at the Audrey, or at a bar just like it—they were all over the Mission and as I've told you, I could never keep them quite straight. He was sitting at a brown vinyl booth with a transvestite named Michael, truly the most abused creature I'd ever seen. You couldn't tell where the bruises stopped under his dress but here he was laughing, and happy, poking with his straw at his drink. The banker had his arms spread over the booth's top, his wrist charm catching light from the wall lamps. For hours, off and on, he gave me the kind of stare a child throws Christmas mornings, when he's torn the wrappings from every present and stands waiting for a gift that will never arrive.

On I-64 west of Evansville I walked the shoulder, not bothering to look back. For three days I'd come south from Ohio, sleeping hidden in the daylight hours and hitching scared down the blacktop at night. At rest stops I broke into cars and I took things. Behind shade trees or dumpsters I waited hours at a time. That night a semi tipped not fifty yards in front of me. It was on the fast side of the two-lane and the median held no rail, just a sunken maw of tanned grass that dipped quickly and efficiently. The semi swerved and caught the edge and lifted itself sideways, crashing. Bumpers and axles dug at the earth. There was a great metallic wailing. Overhead the stars shone, indifferent. It was four in the morning. No cars had passed for close to an hour. I thought about the driver, sleeping forever inside.

The semi's trailer door had opened on impact and amongst the smoke and dust, there in the nighttime, lifted hundreds or thousands of bees. They moved then stood, confused or learning their way from that confusion, but for a short time they were only small things that held moonlight—they were alive and I was alive and we were living. When the buzzing rose up and reached me I was saddened; they had named themselves, and we now had to act accordingly. All around us were cornfields and farther off farmhouses, their porch lights like code on the flatland. The insects pushed on and I kept walking west. The sky was so wide it was startling.

Settlers of Unassigned Lands

I'm behind the old Safeway, the one near the graveyard, where the rigs back in and offload and pull out into the night. I know where to stand so the store clerks can't see me; I know that you stand in the shadows, just under the light. She's coming here to meet me. She's from Oklahoma. I met her at a party, the night before Halloween. Her costume was one of those over-sized fingers and she'd worn it sideways and painted out the team's logo and written on there OK and when I saw it, the first time, the finger looked just like the state I was from.

I took a Greyhound out west, saved up washing dishes, one year of rinsing and scrubbing and lifting, the food I washed off just bloat and hue. Tulsa to Oakland and goodbye tornadoes and here were the Rockies and here the Salt Lake, and there was a man who came into the diner, who drove rig for England and had been saved by the Mormons and knew all their stories, and I said but they thought that that lake was the ocean, and the guy said, but have you seen that lake son, so goodbye to the floodplain, my veins its wrecked roads, the black broken pathways of south Oklahoma, the rare and red earth that soaked up my youth, towns full of gun racks and rig hats and six packs, and Friday night lights, seven to a side because the schools were too small. The train tracks held departure: you could climb in the boxcars, or lie down and wait for the wheels. I knew those who did both, caught out and came back a week after. A day passed, a month passed, then the coroner's low black Hearse would pass by the diner and park next to the spikes, the body, the rails.

Ten years now in Oakland, selling dope to the cute ones, the boys from the parties and these days I'm skinpopping to try and save money, the high longer this way, when you blast up your skin, when you don't shoot the vein and the rush is a lot less but the economy sucks now so the boys, on the weekends, don't come around like they did. My studio's down by the BART at MacArthur, blocks off the strip and the thugged-out per-hours, their parking lots full though you never see people and it's a good place to be, the johns draw the cops' fire, my room just a futon and scales and a table, the big West of small spaces: a wall for a kitchen, a toilet that stands right next to the fridge. But the boys don't come around now, and my rent is past due.

She said she could save me. She said if we fucked, I could make it back home. She said that she knew this was something I wanted. She said she knew I was Okie because I wore my eyes low.

The clerk flicks his butt and pulls the door open and goes back inside and the ember's still smoking and the rigs are all gone and she walks down the alley and she's dyed her hair from blonde to a brown. She's tall. She has white on, a white flowing dress and black motorcycle jacket and I think not yet, I need music inside me, the scene needs its music, this scene needs its score. Past the mouth of the alley, cars blur on Broadway. It's a short walk to the cemetery, where she wants it to happen. At the party she talked of a group of graves there, the bare tiny headstones, the graves without names. They're under a cluster of scrub trees in some grubby corner. The cemetery here in Oakland is huge.

She isn't attractive, or is almost attractive. Her nose is too big and her eyes are too narrow. Her lips do something funny that make her look stupid. Her teeth look too small inside of her mouth. Her hair—there's a term for it—is done up in this wreath; she doesn't have bangs and the front part is braided and she wears these braids pulled back behind her, like the ends of a visor, the braids holding the rest of her long brown hair back. At the party I asked how she knew she could save me, and she told me my play didn't have any actors, and too many directors, and the sets were off-color, and how long had it been since I heard the word supper, the word supper in earnest, used as it should. And it made me believe her: no one out here, in the big West of small spaces, answers questions with questions, and supper's not heard.

She takes my hand and we walk from the alley. The diner I worked at was next to a truck stop, one of those big things that had mainly diesel and the tourists driving through were too scared to stop at, and car washes that only the rig drivers used. I timed my productions to those power washes, the shooting of hoses, the rubbing of shammies against the hard metal truck. I knew how much time I had left by the noises. From the beginning, I did it all with eyes closed. But the boys here were different, there was acceptance, there was commitment on their part to these acts. And some of them loved me, or said that they loved me, and one of them, once, stole most of my drugs, and in the backyard of a party nearly half a year later, I stepped on his kneecap while he stood drinking beer. I shot the bone out and he crumpled and whimpered, and not once more, not ever, were things taken from me. I've been made a fool of but not here, on the coast.

She and I walk by the Wendy's, the tree lot. It's November, and the next week is Thanksgiving: sweaters and slacks and forks, knives and spoons. We're holding hands. She has on black hi-tops. The dope's moving through me like a slow, patient brook. The front of the Safeway is part of a center: there's a café, a store that sells smoothies, a combination pharmacy/every-thing store (and how did we get here and who let this happen and where is the person in all of the meetings on zoning and planning and building and digging who stands up for beauty, who screams in board meetings but what about art but what about art, but what about beauty the need for aesthetic the need for the mind to have things it can question, why is this shaped like this, why is this basic, and where were the dissenters when the men in their ties said it's all about money, fuck art? Because it's graceless. It's graceless to walk with the one who will save you past such tawdry neon, such bright hollow signage, when children are hungry, when graves don't have names. Where is that person, who screams it and screams it, who says no you're wrong, who screams art art art).

The hills near the graveyard harbor thin eucalyptus, the seeds of these trees brought over in the bellies of vermin, the bellies of birds. "How far away is Australia?" I ask her, and she says, *I know what you think now, don't think that I don't.* "But if we build things and these things that are built—like computers, like bridges, like tracks laid for trains, if these things are built to bring us all closer and these things fail to do what they should, then why aren't they torn down? Why don't we start over?"

And she says, *what do you think that it is that I'm trying to do?*

We walk past a steakhouse, a care ward, apartments. The air is thick with the scent of the trees' leaves, and I wonder if Okie has one eucalyptus, if there's even one of these trees in the state that I'm from. I don't know the answer. Perhaps some arboretum. Perhaps some fancy zoo made for flora. Our palms have grown damp from the clasping. I want to let go.

The street tees and down one way, the way all the cars go, is another small district of this big, lonely city, another quaint sector to forget and go shopping and perhaps see a movie and then go get a sundae, and buy for your dog a nice leash made of hemp. To the left is a bar and past it a head-quarters for Oakland's Hells Angels and beyond that the vaults and white-walled mausoleum, across the street from which stands a small flower shop. We walk past the bar and its door is open and the din flares like rash or a bite from a spider, and I want to tell her there's no way I can do this, let's just forget it, I'm not going out there, to the place where they bury those who have no one, and she tells me *if all of those people had no one then there wouldn't be graves there* and I want so badly the boys who all love me, the ones who come over past midnight and skinpop, the best high for fucking, the high building with sweating, with lips that I kiss with a sad sort of panic, as the truckers did not want to be kissed at all, and my small apartment with glass-topped coffee table and futon and bed sheets and sometimes a post-card from Brother in Tulsa, where he works as a banker and has now three children, and remains a Baptist, and calls me deserter, but does not know enough of the truth to say *faggot*, the word he would use if he had to use one, and I don't want to go there, to the graves with no names.

The columbarium's dark. It's well past business hours. Behind its walls are rows of gold boxes, and each of these boxes hold peoples' ashes, and these boxes of ashes are all kept in columns, and the rooms all have fountains and the rooms all have names. I dress nice when I come here: I own two sweaters; I own two pairs of gray pinstriped pants. I watch them sometimes, the victims, the living: they read the dead poems, they leave bouquets in holders. They are scared to forget because the dead can't remember. They are scared because all of the boxes aren't full.

She and I climb the gate; I hoist her over spires, over wrought iron points like a row of short pikes. She drops down and her white dress parachutes upward, a broken umbrella, taken by wind. She told me her name at the party we met at. She has the same name as my mother, my bright, dying mother, who must surely know. We look at each other through the black iron bars and the nighttime. There's a street light behind me, in front of the small flower shop. She looks like a child; her cheeks are too pudgy. She looks like she can't be a person at all. *Climb over, climb over*, she says, *do you want me to help you.*

But I don't need her help now. I can do it myself.

The roads in the graveyard go on for miles. Past the gate is a six-foot porcelain urn. Behind it the road breaks into four curving fingers. At the top of the graveyard are more eucalyptus, new marble headstones, fresh even sod. There's a view of The City, a place I've not been to. I don't own a car and am scared of the subway: it goes underwater, it's like Oklahoma, the asphalt on floodplain, the water above. The sink at the diner had a spray washer that hung down like the head of a shower, and I remember its weight, its spring-loaded tug. If you pulled then let go, it was like a man hanging: it would bounce and then bounce and then sway and then stop. Tonight there are stars and not much pollution and long smears of white on the black vacant cosmos. Her dress looks like a ghost as she moves up the road. The cemetery here is three-hundred acres. There's Millionaires' Row, its piedmont of tombs, names above doors forever and ever, and buried here is the man who founded Folgers' Coffee, and buried here is Kaiser, the man who built ships, and buried here are sculptors and sheriffs and judges, and painters and mayors, and the man known as the father of hydraulic mining, as patriarch of employing water to dislodge solid rock, and how did he think that water could do this, was he from Oklahoma, did he see the floodplain, did he work in a diner, washing off ketchup from dishes, and she's walking faster than I am and stops, and says that we have to go all the way to the top, that the graves without names and the small grove of scrub trees are on the backside of the cemetery lot, and she takes off her jacket and leaves it in the gutter, and her skin looks so pink against the dress's white fabric that I think for a moment that she's made out of gum.

When I was young and okay and the world still cost nothing, my family, in summer, went north to Nebraska, to a town not that far from the South Dakota line. There was a lake there, a college, a church with round skylight. An uncle had a cabin, a jet ski, a pier. We swam until sunburned. An elm grew from the shoreline, and from one of its limbs, and by rope, hung a tire, and I broke my leg the last summer I went there, by not letting go, by watching the water and shore moving backward, the dirt rushing upward, the string of poor choices. My brother was with me. I lay there panting. Do you want me to get mom or should I stay here with you. My brother moved toward me and lifted me up and put me on his shoulder and half-carried, half-dragged me back to the cabin, where my family's faces fell down like horses, their shock meaning love.

I remember the dice on one trucker's mirror. I remember my father asking of girls. I remember the boys, the long nights and candles, the dope on the table, the smooth plastic lust. I am to have a small place in some history, but this place exists without any tradition, and history absent of any tradition is a coat without buttons, a bird without call. A dry dying floodplain I can't not remember. She leaves the roadside and angles her body and walks sideways, in white dress, down the leaf-covered hill. By the back of the fence, in the moonlight, I see them, the grave without names, like small silver huts. Most of my life has been filled with these items, myself as a settler of unassigned lands. I function as permanent, illegal homesteader. I have built houses but these houses aren't mine now. I miss Oklahoma. The nights don't get hot here. I miss the dim wetness, the minor insistence of moisture in air. The warm smell of crop dirt when the storm's lifted. The blank stare of cattle. The rare and red earth.

The Ledge

and the streets lined with maples and meters and cars, the fall streets and winter streets and dirty-hot streets of deep summer, when everyone went out, when lameness prevailed and the yuppies wore shorts and bought saris for uncultured loved ones, and the record stores were too full and the bookstores too full and there was only the corner store, where he went for his cigarettes, with its battered linoleum and impossible selection of foods—pasta and relish and beef stew and chocolate chips—the corner store which he still goes to but only at night now, just before it closes, where the Turkish man, stoic, waits on his stool, the Turkish man with his nose hair and bent glasses frames, the Turkish man who has told him that he was a *structural engineer after college*, which he doesn't believe, because if you are a structural engineer then you own a watch of titanium and a summer house in Squaw Valley and you do not wear glasses like he wears, and you do not run a corner store where your kids crawl on the counter like lemurs, and if the Turkish man was truly a structural engineer then the world was a hellscape of lucklessness, which was what he believed in the stone pit of his heart, and on the wall behind the counter the phone cards for Africa, and who bought those.

and the college town and those friends and those years ago, and Central Time and the beige hum of cicadas, and maybe a song could sum it all up, he can't remember, he has eighteen plastic crates filled with records, won't buy cds, the sound isn't warm, the sound isn't accurate, but the Midwest, back then, the attic room of a house, and bats lived in the walls the whole winter: there was the shell of the house then the shell of the room and between them, in those inches, the bats lived, and the claws on their wings made sounds when they moved, a scratching that seemed to denote sickness, and the mattress on the ground and the girlfriend he loved and the girls that he fucked and loved also, drunk always, all of them, the dirt roads and corn fields and the clouds on the horizon, and the moon rang with its ring of faeries, and how did the moon and how did the bats and how did they drink and get on and buy food and have jobs and cry and laugh also, and where are these people because he can't find them now, has tried to, has typed their names into websites where you typed your name into websites and put pictures up with your own likeness, and listed off miserably your favorite things, and your favorite people, a million shrines like these, a million intangible temples of ego, and not one person that he once knew inside them.

but now the thirties, the crush of the future, the onset of make-it-or-break-it, when one bought leather shoes and stopped smoking pot and chose a job that was like all the others, a job drenched in swipe cards and passwords and mouse pads (and Theta, the buildings were awful, the windows fractured the light and robbed it of warmth, the windows did not even open); horrible, useless, patronizing jobs, jobs that bored men to baldness, the earth of their brains depleted of food until the blades of their hair furtively loosed and washed through the grate of the shower drain, jobs built around a fervent, pornographic belief in the Federal Reserve System, in taxes of income, in which people voluntarily chose to be slaves, and someone, it was Goethe, had a quote about that, not about taxes but being a slave, and that the best kind of slave was an unwitting one, and he was paraphrasing now and did this make him a slave, and why was it called a 1040, and to counter this servitude *these jobs came with benefits:* protection of vision, protection of teeth, protection of one's miles of intestine, so that one could thank god it was Friday with coworkers in sports bars, could drink draft beer and watch hockey and this was applauded, was encouraged, because if something went wrong and you got fat or sick, you'd bought in and someone would fix you, and you could go back to the sports bar and get sick again—jobs that included stock options, and these were options that one had to have, and if one existed without options of stock then one's future was a hellscape of lucklessness, and the smells that pervaded one's next forty years were not car leather, cologne or scallops pan-seared, not mountain air, beach air or lake air, but those of patchouli and cat urine, the peasant spices of the line striker, the smells of the left, smells that connoted a substantial lack of purchasing power, and implied a beard and ownership of a Schwinn and that you thought of the suburbs as death camps.

and every month in the mailbox more invitations, on eggshell or ivory card-stock, their fonts calligraphic, die cast embossed, please join us, please join us, please honor us, and he touched at the ridges, felt the depressions, moved his hand like the blind reading Braille, and the parties were always at places he loathed and that they said that they loathed but then supported: country clubs with duck sauce and alabaster-hued linens, and fairways for golf, and swan-shaped ice sculptures, and the ice swans were stunning and he wanted to touch them or at least just stand there admiring, but they were not to be looked at or at least not examined, not to be thought of in a critical context—they were ornament, strictly, purchased and centered and trans-ferred to chips housed in digital cameras, where the ice swan, long gone, was immortal, was not water then dew drops and then condensation, and then fog that hung in a valley, and covered the maples and meters and streets in a deep morning silence, a fog that the senders of the invitations *hoped would burn off by go-time*, a fog that was somehow unlucky, and contained in its vapor the corpses of millions of previous ice swans, a fog that the bride and groom didn't want hanging around while they said their oaths then their toasts then their thank-yous, and packed up their gifts and boarded a plane and spent a week fucking in a honeymoon suite and no matter how badly he needed the cash he was always late to return his tuxedo.

and then more invitations, the bellies of strangers, *tumescent as springtime chrysalides*, and these were the wives, the well-kempt Anglo-Saxons, the lisas and lauras and kellys, and when they answered the doors of their subur-ban homes, he watched their faces with a microscope's scrutiny, looking to see, in those milliseconds, the change from fear to full understanding, dur-ing which he, in the minds of the wives, was transformed completely, from black thug and rapist and where's my cell phone to *coworker of the person I married*, and the doors opened wider, were swung open fully, and his coat was hung up and he said his hellos and sometimes the wives, shot through with guilt, overcompensated and kept bringing him things, and there was the time that he got the house number wrong, that he rang the wrong house's doorbell, and this was in evening, full nighttime outside, and when he told the woman, fear choking her throat, that he was sorry and must be mistaken, she said that she thought that he must be right, and shut the door while he stood there, which was followed by the deadbolt thrown into the lock, and the scraping of the chain on the wooden door's backside, and these actions had made him laugh uncontainably, as he stared at the doormat that said WELCOME; and this in turn proceeded by the walk to the car he had borrowed and the *continued navigation of suburbia*, and then the police, and please exit the vehicle, and the rest was just a scene from a movie, but in his coworker's houses the wives pulled up their shirts and showed to him navels near bursting, and they grabbed at his arms and placed his palms on their skin and said touch it, just put your hand there.

and he loved to skateboard and was skating now, rode goofy, could kick flip, could manage with ease the steel rails of stairways outside of government buildings, and in backpack and black sweatshirt and filthy white jeans was heading south, toward the border of Berkeley and Oakland, where they had mauled Stein's quote about the latter of these towns the way that public art so aptly mauled everything, past the bronze here, past the bronze there, each letter block and taller than he was, south down Martin Luther King Boulevard, and now Oakland, Bump City, the place where he'd grown up, the place with the highest crime rate in California, home of black panthers and the angels of hell, home of Bruce Lee's very first dojo, and the pavement was new and the wheels rolled in silence, very near glided, and he had a tweed cap on, and out past the airport, over toward Hayward, East Oakland, enormous, a war zone; *a living cemetery*, one publication had called it, and here were the ghosts of dead rappers and the men who had killed them, and in turn were killed by the friends of dead rappers, who in turn were killed by the men's friends, and so on; and the shuttered and broken factory windows—gone was Granny Goose, gone was Gerber—and this area, until 1909, had been known as *Brooklyn*, which made total sense to him, was across from the glow and the flare of the City, was separated by bridge, by water, except *this* part of *this* city would never ascend, would never be pretty or rich or anything more than the part of the city one hoped to never step foot in, the part of the city that had not seen a spike in development *since prior to the bombing of Dresden,* and in recent years was most famous for its crack epidemic, and Felix Mitchell (and Theta do you remember the day of his funeral, we must have been ten or eleven, and people lined the streets to look at the casket, and Huey Newton was there and Rolls Royce limousines, along with a procession of ten horse-drawn carriages, because this guy was a kingpin who had given back, who sold crack and then built children playgrounds, which we played on, and when these are your zip code's and neighborhood's heroes, Theta, it kind of fucks with your sense of morality), and with Felix Mitchell's stabbing and death inside Leavenworth Prison came a sudden and drastic reduction in cost *of producing cocaine in rock form* in Oakland, and the east side in turn became a market destabilized, and then just an orgy of violence, the police chief agog, the paramedics like overworked janitors, and here were the sysdeshows along east 14th, the cars of the grinders spinning in circles, and leaving on the lots' asphalt circles of skid marks, and the circle as infinity, as closed simple curves, as existing without entrance or exit.

and with the honeycombed sole of his canvas hi-top he now steers the board down 53rd st., toward the old Victorian he's lived in eight years, with its pink scalloped siding and bowed wooden porch and brocaded curtains hung over the windows, the whimsical two-level with untended yard of crab grass and deadening Albas, a house emblematic of civic upkeep's patina, a house filled with renters and bedrooms, where hillocks of mail sprang from the sill of the foyer's tall picture window, and stains left on the wall behind the four-burner stove had altered the wall's very color, and lent a mélange that paid tribute to literally hundreds of meals of pasta, the long-hardened dots of maroon-colored sauce like a mind's eye picture-game puzzle, dots representing the culinary exploits of residents both past and current, the meek indie hipsters and long-haired metalheads and post-feminist vegan subversives, who had seen the ad listed in the local free paper, and needed something short term, and affordable, and could move in if possible like maybe this week—people from other parts of the country, who had left what they'd known and fled for the coast, and its climate of progressive tranquility, where their futures were not linked to price shifts in cattle, were not dependent upon fluctuations in the bentonite industry, and they might never see, again in their lives, the outline of a grain elevator, might not be called fag in the bathrooms of bars, their forehead put hard against the urinal's porcelain, departed places like Carbondale and Miles City, Montana, the coach's big wheels spitting gravel, and got to the Bay and played lead guitar in a band that no one had heard of, and when someone moved out, their narrative lost, someone else moved in on the heels of them, and in this way the story was epic in scope, contained verse upon verse upon chorus, and there was the art student who tattooed herself, and there was the girl that dressed like Zelda Fitzgerald, and the software designer and political aide and the bulimic Latina fire eater, and the throngs of wage slaves working doubles in aprons, chopping fennel at some kitchen's station, and when the dinner rush came they plated up squab or risotto topped with shavings of truffle, then repaired to back alleys for low-tar cigarettes and bitched and cajoled and vowed always to quit and could because *all this was temporary*, because they could get new jobs and rent other rooms in still other Victorians, and join for a short while some other tribe of momentarily lingering nomads, who spoke dialects that were nearly their own, or close enough to foster understanding, and at night past his window the whistle of trains, headed eastbound, back toward the heartland.

and with the skateboard abandoned he ascends the porch steps and produces a key from his pocket, and the smell there to greet him in the cluttered foyer is the musk most common to the house's interior, the scent of *cooked pasta*, boiled in a pot, then dumped in a colander hung from the faucet, a smell as common to the house's inside as cut grass is in the suburbs, and on the bare floor of the near empty living room someone sitting on a rust-colored beanbag, watching the eight-inch Hitachi, the set appearing over winter on the top of the room's only bookcase, black-and-white and rabbit-eared and with the capacity to pick up exactly two stations, a local affiliate and the public broadcasting channel, and he has no idea if the guy on the beanbag is a guest or a tenant, or is involved with the boiling of the pasta, and hung at odd angles with wire and nails, *art in a wide range of mediums*, paper collage and acrylic on canvas and found objects that had been spray-painted: the red of a stop sign done over in green, dolls set on fire then covered in lipstick; and paintings condemning the eating of meat, and paintings condemning all manner of consumption, that spoke out against, in ways complex and basic, the idea of commodity fetishism, *art largely Marxist in nature*, and this was ironic as nearly all of the art had been bought at the local flea market, and thereby debased what it sought to uphold, namely the belief of a social relationship, one that existed outside of the shackles of the Federal Reserve System, and its printing of fake paper currency, and its concurrent demanding of a tax on income, a tax based on the ignorance of this country's masses, a tax not supported by one single phrase contained in the U.S. Constitution, and from the tiny Hitachi a scripted game show: *are you going to go for it? Bob, I'm going to go for it*, and the guy on the beanbag saying *you fucking zombies.*

and why he is here, what's brought him by (because really he is here very little, works six days a week at a local bookstore where they pay him well under the table, and had said in the interview prior to hiring that he would only take the job if he didn't have to fill out a 1040, and thereby avoid the illegal taxation of any and all future wages, which had happened when he had worked in an office, and the bookstore's owner was a pony-tailed man from the suburb of Short Hills, New Jersey, a septuagenarian who *did* own a Schwinn and *did* carry about him the odor of cat urine, and this man had gotten a gleam in his eye at the mention of opposing the 1040, and instead of saying no and thanks for your time shook his hand and said you start tomorrow), is the book kept in a lockbox hidden under his bed, and the book there is none other than the big book of AA, fourth edition, the faux leather binding not quite navy blue and he's had this book now for over five years, since a little after his firing from the job that he held at the office, the termination occurring when on a Friday he had *urinated on a plant by the water cooler*, when he'd come back from a late lunch had with coworkers, who unlike him had not been covertly drinking vodka all morning, and who had not been drinking vodka the evening before, and for every night for four years before that; who did not need the vodka to physically function, and thereby stave off the invisible beast known as *delirium tremens,* from which one's head spun and wrists felt hollowed out, which transformed the mundane or simplistic chore to near-mythic proportions, and it was only after the daily slaying of this beast that the first thoughts of food were really possible, and that day, that Friday, by three o'clock, he was amazingly hungry because he was *shit-faced,* because he had filled a Dixie cup with Smirnoff for six hours straight, and now felt pretty good about things, felt well enough to realistically consider the thorough mastication of spring rolls, and since it was Friday a beer with his lunch fell in the realm of acceptable, and here were his coworkers at his cubicle's threshold, the expats of Beta house chapters, the Aryan trust-funders who owned lacrosse sticks and on weekends wore piqued, collared Izods, and for now were living in *secure-entranced townhouses in the Lake Merritt area of Oakland*, and how did Thai food sound to him; and then the elevator's descent and the gift of fresh air and the bringing of menus to their table, and the measured expert nursing of one single brown bottle of beer of southeast Asian extraction, and when the spring rolls arrived he eagerly ate as this was his lunch and his breakfast and dinner, and would allow for, at some point in the very near future, the continued consumption of vodka, and the Beta house expats spoke of Oakland's crime rates, and asked him again where it was that he did his college.

and by just after five the office was empty—it was a Friday in springtime—and he sat there reclined with the Dixie cup, then put the glass bottle of vodka inside his book bag and switched off his desk's computer, and as he was leaving lingered a moment in front of *the large potted silver queen,* unzipping the fly of his khakis, the drive of this action unfolding from the nihilistic imbibing of Smirnoff, and as urine hit soil the elevator bell dinged, and this was the boss's return from a board meeting, and this boss was in her 50s and an Ivy League MBA and had at Choate and then at Brown gone by the nickname of Binky (now: Rebecca), and drove a Lexus sedan and didn't take shit, and had never seen anyone urinating in a planter in a hallway, but was transported immediately to her freshman dorm room and her own bout, as she called it, of poor decision-making, during which she had invited up to her room a *scholarship student* from Hartford's inner city, and this *scholarship student* didn't know when to stop and had forcibly undone her bra strap, and pinched at her nipples and put his hand up her skirt with the measured force, his boss said, of industrial machinery, of something inhuman performing a task, and she had leaned back on the bed and had kicked him, and he'd gotten up and flashed her the peace sign, and the next four years of her life she kept seeing him, and saw him in dreams, and saw him when waking, reworking the scene on the stage of her brain over and over and over, all of this flooding back, she had said, as she stared at his stream of urine, which ceased upon his recognition of the person who held tightly the purse strings, and inside her office, behind the maple-stained door, the silver queen recounting that Providence night, then saying *here's what we're going to do: I'll pay you out for another two months and you don't come back here, not once, not ever.*

and then the writing of the check and giving over of swipe cards, his shame very near to congealing, and the next fifty sixty or seventy days were akin to a device in screenwriting, where the screenwriter must show that much time has passed, and must do so rather quickly, so that the audience gets a sense of time passing *only through glimpses,* and these glimpses, were they specific to him, might show a black kid alone in the bedroom he rented and a futon encircled by bottles, and records lying flat on their white paper sleeves, which in turn rested on record covers, and ashtrays erupting with clumps of tan butts, and night and day passing unnoticed, and the stirring of the black kid, on some random May date, at four seventeen in the morning, and thinking the single word vodka, and sitting up from the bed and check-ing the bottles, etc., ad nauseum; and then the abated eating of food, the mitigation of solids and subsequent vomiting, until the feel of bile corrod-ing his teeth became rather standard—a series of scenes pieced together with washouts, a cinematic collage bathetically steeped in addiction, and then the waking one morning to the cadence of finches, and deciding to throw out the bottles, and with the bottles thrown out the grim meeting rooms of the hopelessly lost and delusional, of the drunk who had turned his life over, and here were the worn dirty floors of church basements and the aroma of crystallized French roast, and if you need a sponsor please raise your hand, and that we alcoholics cannot manage our lives and that god could and would once we sought him, and that first year an epiphany, a deep cleansing breath, and he did get a sponsor and then his sponsor moved and then he found a new sponsor, a subcontractor, a libertarian, who informed him of the lie that was income tax, and told him to work the steps harder, and then had a heart attack in the cab of his Ford (and with death conquered fully his addiction), and all that was over a year ago, and since the death of this sponsor his own attendance at the Monday ten-thirty had dwindled, and then ceased entirely, and tonight wouldn't be any different, because where he is going involves no house of worship but does in some ways consider the fourth step, *the taking of a personal inventory,* and with the box locked and room locked he then leaves the house, skating slowly south, out toward the ghetto.

(because Theta there are so many ledges to manage—narrow and shelf-like, projecting—that the concept of structure is all but lost among all of this balancing, and there are so many parts I can locate no sum, and there seems to me no way to solve this equation, and on a bench in a Laundromat someone reading a book, as next door in a pawn shop a man pleads with the clerk, and at the intersection of Macarthur the filthy motels and slicked glow of fast food enterprises, and the hookers (all black) done up with drugs, and fake eyelashes bought from a Walgreen's, and Theta, dear twin sister of mine, I want you to know I'm wearing the cap that you sent me last Christmas, the one made of wool with the snap on its bill, *the derby of cream and tan herringbone*, and sister in truth the cap fits rather poorly, and how is the suburb of Arlington Heights, your village northwest of Chicago, is it the same as it was when I came to visit, and met your white husband and my nephew and niece, and breathed in the air that fills your tax bracket, and saw parked in your driveway the green Cherokee and sleek white Mustang convertible, and Theta I know a surgeon's hours are long, that the man that you married, while married to you, is married to the work he does also, and what do *you* do, twin sister, all day in that house, while your kids get called ugly names at their grade school, and what will you do when you take your kids downtown and they begin to more fully comprehend where this country keeps its surfeits of black people, because I know you remember when one of your suburb's cops saw us walking last autumn near sunset, and turned his car down the street and then matched our gait, the cop rolling down the car window, asking could he help us—asking us, twin sister, *if we were lost*, to which I replied *almost certainly*, after which the cop applied his car's brakes, and Theta do you just shrug this off all the time, build it in to the cost of your gabled Tudor.)

and toward Oakland's downtown the turn on to West Grand and ahead of him *damned tidal waters*, where a convergence of streams greets the bay's gray saline, and creates the brackish lagoon named Lake Merritt: an urban lake, a lake surrounded by a city, a lake at one point used as a grave for the corpses of gang members, their wrecked bodies pulled from the dark trunks of cars and dragged over the grass to the shoreline—a cruel task performed in the heart of the night (and Theta do you remember how the applications *cost?* that there were processing fees and we had no money?), a task done with urgency, the legs lifted first, grabbed just above the black hi-tops, legs left to rest on the chrome of the bumper while the body's torso and shoulders were worked on, and this taking time as the body was stuck, was wedged up against the spare tire, and then purchase gained with a yank on the neck, and the body in turn rolling over (and Theta has your surgeon husband told you that a corpse harbors breath long after the lungs have stopped working, because at times, on good days, I can forget his face—the scar on his jaw, the uneven sideburns—but what won't go away is the scent of that breath, an odor matching exactly *cooked pasta*, and I wonder sometimes about his last meal's specifics—did he sit at a table, was he watching TV, did he finish eating and then use a napkin, some thin paper thing that he crumpled up, telling a brother or sister of his own, *I'm going out, I'll see you later*, which he wouldn't), the air filled in by fog, the body exhaling postmortem, and with another pull the body toppling out of the trunk, half on the street and half on the sidewalk, sprawling grotesquely over the gutter then dragged over sod that was covered in goose shit, and rolled from the ped path and into the lake's lapping water, as the instructions had been to *not* weigh the corpse, as the instructions had been WE WANT MOTHER-FUCKERS TO *KNOW* US, and twin sister you should see what the lake looks like now, how pretty it is, how it has strings of lights strung around it.

and with the shoreline beside him the backpack unzipped, the skateboard not losing momentum, and here the drawing out of two things at once, the big book of AA and a can of malt liquor, the six-pack bought from the Turkish man just before closing and the former thrown into the water, gone forever, the cheap glue of its binding dissolving, the faux leather covers, not quite navy blue, fanned out and now slightly bobbing, as he pops the can's top then pedals faster, around the ped path to the west side of the lake, past the Beta house expats and their slumbering wives, past the dreaming lisas, lauras, and kellys, who've been assured by their husbands a house in the suburbs, and their own toddler toddling, who know just like he does that down East 14th lie all manner of problems—that this street heads south for miles—runs past 29th and the tidal canal and the bridges that connect Alameda, runs past the braid shops and bus stops and dark dirty bars, runs just west of his decrepit alma mater, that high school where he spent four years of his life while living with six different relatives, in six differ-ent houses, an institution to which he was bused fifty blocks because his neighborhood had no high school to speak of, was south of the airport and sports coliseums and the warehouses' wrecked broken windows, a locale with main streets sometimes traversed by one or both of his parents, in the years post-Felix Mitchell, a time when crack was much cheaper, a time when his neighborhood was an open-air market for the selling of cocaine in rock form, a market that's still alive to this day, a market that's very much thriving, and twin sister since this is your story, too, do you remember see-ing them from out of the bus window, the people who raised us, who once had had jobs and owned cars and paid in to the Federal Reserve System, and then didn't, as there weren't any more jobs to have, as industry flat-lined and they got their pink slips, and if life is a ledge then here the mis-step, the loss of all balance, and the appearance of grim men on our porch in the nighttime, men wearing black sateen Raiders jackets, and one car was sold then the other, the cupboards bare and lawn dead and then disappear-ance, the absences longer and longer, until a CPS agent showed up with a clipboard and *juice boxes*, because we were malnourished and now pity cases, and repaired that very day to an uncle's, and Theta was it maybe once every three weeks that the bus would drive past them, our parents, as they searched through a trash can or smoked in an alley, and how many times did they show up at the home of an aunt and hug us and then steal money, or food stamps they'd sell to the corner store owners at a highly depreciated value, because food stamps cannot buy *cocaine in rock form* but hard cash is fiscally omniscient, and with cash one can pay rent or buy drugs or a six-pack of tall cans of malt liquor, and with cash one can stand in line at the post office, looking at mug shots of felons, and wait to exchange three hun-dred in twenties for ten different money orders, to five different colleges, institutions that promised, in so many words, we'll give you money if you give us money, meaning, twin sister, there were *processing fees*, and surely at some point you put this together, that the money didn't come from an uncle or aunt or employ of our school district, that if we were us (and sister, are we?) and seventeen and past poor and quickly in need of three hundred dollars, there was one demographic to turn to, and this demographic could be found oftentimes on a roof out on 98th Avenue—a roof that I'm now heading back to—and were happy to part with some of their funds if in turn one did them a favor, because Theta hard cash is *the key of the skeleton*, and there are so many doors it can open.

and sister the doors that it opened for us—the first black twins in our college's history—and how many times were we asked by those friends I can't find *so who's the good one and who's the bad one*, and Theta for me the jury's still out, and you really should write home more often, because those uncles and aunts never went anywhere, and they clothed and fed us, and right now a plane going by overhead, the sound of its engines enormous, a sound that could fill up your suburb's quaint silence, would mask wholly the hum of your pool filter, a timbre entirely afforded to you by my disposal of *a victim of gang members*, men met on a roof over ten years ago at an hour very near this one, and who lived in the walls of my attic room, and on every dirt road and in every cornfield—lived everywhere, Theta, in all that I saw, were sewn into my vision's fabric, and for me stand always on the flat granite top of a long-closed Grocery Outlet, and Theta I'm sorry for so much disclosure but in some ways you were always unlucky, left-handed and clumsy, the dog that Mom bought you run over, your best friend from third grade shot accidentally, also a victim of gang members, and Theta it seems implied by your actions that you're not interested too much in history, but you should know that your name, the eighth letter in Greek, was used by *judges Hellenic*, and that in ancient times these men wrote down this letter when prescribing death under penalty, and I'm sure that our parents just heard it somewhere and knew nothing of its implications, were unaware it dealt largely with closure and doom, and also with stock options, as your name, twin sister, in regard to investing, is a measure of *the decaying of options*, that as time progresses decay tends to grow, and will keep growing larger and larger, until expiration, and Theta I'm now out on 91st Avenue, where the rate of decay is unchartable, where the stone edge of this city wakes up and looks at itself and sees only a hellscape of lucklessness, where the streets are not lined with maples and meters and cars because there's no soil for trees to grow in, and the meters have all had a hacksaw taken to them, so that addicts can get at their quarters, and cars parked here past midnight are gone before morning, stolen and taken to chop shops, and the church lots' chain-links are all topped with barbed wire, and there's not one single bookstore to speak of, just corner stores, gas stations, and check-cashing places, and a black kid riding a skateboard, and shifting his weight and steering the board into the mouth of an alley, the pavement gone rougher, a beer can thrown down, the board's wheels coughing out bits of gravel, and Theta, it's quiet, there's no one around, and half of my tall boys have yet to be opened, and here are my hands on the fire ladder's rungs, and here is the roof of this building, so answer me, sister: if you have falling dreams, too, what is it you do to wake yourself from them.

The Subject of Our First Issue Is Art

She lived next to the train tracks, but there were rarely trains—all of the lines that came through at one time had been rerouted. Now, though, a short one passed by: just an engine pulling two silver tubes, followed by a small gray caboose. She waved from behind the warehouse's windows. The conductor didn't wave back. She wondered what the tubes might contain. She didn't know where the tracks led save that they went east, out past the LACTMA yard and over the river. She'd followed them once but ran into some friends sitting at a café and talked to them for a while and the friends asked her to go to a gathering in Monterey Park: some med student with tanks full of ether. So she went. For her, this was how LA worked—all of its mysteries, its vague intrigues, ended at mediocre parties.

The train passed and she turned back around. The interviewer was German. He was flying in from Berlin. Her paintings were up, as were the screens for the video projectors. There'd been lightning storms over JFK, and the interviewer's connection had been delayed, the date pushed back from yesterday to today. She'd had to call into work, to say no to a movie that paid very well and was to start shooting that evening. What was the interviewer's name? Maybe Franz. Maybe Fritz. She'd put him in her phone as INTERVIEWER. The magazine was new, but he'd said distribution would be good. The subject of their first issue was art. She was wearing a butter-yellow cotton jersey dress, baby blue thigh highs, and mint green ballet flats that she'd bought for a dollar at the Universal Church of Christ rummage sale. Her hair was bright white. It had taken some work. But now it looked stunning, like chalk, like summer clouds. She'd given herself bangs Thursday night, maybe Friday morning.

She traipsed through the warehouse, arms at her sides. The space had four bedrooms, one built out from each wall. No one had been home since the party, which had started on Thursday and lasted past dawn and then past noon, and then had kept going through Friday night, a new wave of attendees with fresh blood and more drugs arriving. It came back in scenes: a fight out on the street, a kid's red plastic beach pail full of cocaine, Monique in a gold blouse and silver high heels, laughing, screaming her pants had gone missing. She'd cleaned up some: washed off a few plates, put bottles of wine and hard alcohol in the recycling. Someone, perhaps her, had written SLUT on the bathroom mirror in neon pink lipstick. She'd wiped this word off. What had the fight been about, she wondered.

The room's ceiling was eleven feet tall. Rows of recessed lights glowed softly. She walked back toward her bedroom and stared at the strands of teak beads that hung over its threshold. The walls of the space were painted in pastels: mint and peach and soft blue and lavender. The kitchen was recessed along the west wall. Its twin windows looked down at the train tracks and alley. On the floor by the stove was a purple metallic boa. The boa belonged to Dannell—the party had been in his honor. He'd done all the makeup for a low-budget film that had premiered on the Sci-Fi Channel the night of the party. In it, a group of teens were attacked over and over by zombie pterodactyls. Some of the makeup had looked very good, but the film was low-fi, the CGI poor. She herself had been in films with better effects than those in the pterodactyl movie.

Dannell had a piece of shimmery white fabric over the threshold of his bedroom. She said his name then peeked in. All of his stuff was gone: his makeup case, his dresser and mattress. She realized now—remembered, she guessed—that the fight on the street was Dannell's final exit. She'd bought the warehouse five years ago, when she was twenty-three, and rented out rooms at below-market rates to people she in some way found interesting. One of the space's only firm rules was that none of the porn she was in could be shown in the residence. It was fine if they watched her and she didn't find out, but if the films were ever broadcast when she was around, or if she could hear one of her movies playing from someone's bedroom, that person was gone, no thirty days notice. Dannell had broken this rule during the party. She'd been in her bedroom with Monique and another girl, Lindsay. Lindsay was an intern up at the Getty, nineteen and from Chicago somewhere, one of its suburbs filled with shade trees and money. She and Monique had been getting Lindsay high, chopping up lines of ecstasy on the glass over one of Monique's family photos. She'd thought it in bad taste but Lindsay was awed and already drunk, and her body was perfect. The girl had her bra off when the movie came on and her smile dropped off her face and she'd walked out of her bedroom and into the party, where *Latex Empire* was being played on one of the projectors. Dannell was watching the movie with two people she didn't know, all three of them laughing and pointing. He saw her and smiled and waved. She'd walked into the kitchen, where she found Golem and Pope, both of them in black pants and black t-shirts and black bomber jackets. The two men worked security at some of her sets and then hired themselves out as muscle at parties. One of them—Golem, she thought—had once been on TV, in a pay-per-view mixed martial arts competition.

She'd turned the kitchen's corner and walked right into Pope's chest, the two men having heard the movie themselves and on their way to turn it off and find out who did it. Golem was from Prague. Pope was from Bogotá.

"Who?" Golem asked.

She pointed at Dannell. "Him," she had said. "Purple boa." Both men had blinked once, not saying a word, and then walked past her. Golem had picked Dannell up by his face. Dannell put both his hands on Golem's arm, his legs swinging as Golem carried him through the party and then down the stairs. Pope turned off the movie and followed them. Some of the partygoers trailed behind; the rest went back to talking and dancing. She'd walked into the kitchen and looked out the window, down at the alley that the train tracks passed through. Dannell lay in a ball on the concrete. Golem and Pope were hitting him with burlap sacks filled with flour. They brought these bags to the parties they worked; the sacks didn't leave marks, but they did break ribs and lent concussions. The beating went on for ten seconds, then more, Dannell's thin body flattening out as he lost consciousness. A guy in a silver suit and black pinstriped shirt appeared next to her, at the window. Pope hit Dannell again and the sack of flour burst open.

"Holy shit, is that coke?" the guy asked. "Is this a movie or something?"

She walked into the kitchen and opened the fridge. A gore-stained human head stared out at her. Her heart jumped in her chest. She calmed down and stuck out her finger and touched at the head. Its nose fell off; underneath were layers of cake and butter cream. She was upset that she'd hurt the dessert; she had no idea who'd brought it to the party. She closed the fridge door and looked again at the boa. Golem or Pope must have brought it back in—some proof of earning their keep, which rang in at one hundred an hour.

She sat down by the door that led downstairs. The ground floor of the building was full of office chairs; sometimes, a van came and took chairs away, or brought more chairs to store there. Earlier that day, she'd found Lindsay's phone number next to her pillow. She hadn't been to the Getty for two years, at least. Maybe she'd call Lindsay and they'd go get lunch. She'd like to see what the girl looked like outside, in some toned-down skirt under a blue sky and slipstream. Her cell phone chirped; the interviewer had landed. The text read *LAX, need address, one hour*. She texted back where she lived and then *see you soon*. She walked to the bathroom and looked at herself in the mirror. A small smudge of pink lipstick still clung to the glass. She stuck her thumb to the surface and scraped off the pink but in doing so left behind her thumbprint. She tugged up her thigh highs and walked out of the bathroom, pausing to look at her paintings. The canvases were big, 30×40. There were seven paintings in the series. She had titles for none. The canvases were covered with paper inserts taken from her porn DVDs. She'd painted over the inserts with Easter tones, the same ones she'd painted the warehouse walls with. There was something the series was in need of still, but she didn't know what, didn't know how to fix it.

She decided that it would be a smoking week. She hadn't had a smoking week for some time, and she liked the idea of smoking while she was interviewed. She walked down the stairs and then out the door, entering the combination for the lock that sat over the parking lot gate's handle. The combination was her mom's birthday. She pushed the lock's base up and it opened. She looked down the alley, toward the river, and then down toward Fifth. There were two different stores she went to, to get booze and cigarettes, and these stores were the same distance from her warehouse, almost down to the footstep. Through the open window, upstairs, she heard her cell phone ring. She guessed that it was her agent, Marianne, calling back. Marianne was a plump woman in her mid-fifties. She had bobbed platinum hair and wore sensible suits that she bought off the rack at mall outlets. She looked like an overweight soccer mom, which she was: she drove a white Volkswagen minivan, was a mother of three, had a husband who worked in auto insurance. Marianne voted Republican and had an enormous collection of guns. She'd hemmed and hawed about changing her contract to strictly girl–girl, as Marianne, in her personal life, condemned homosexuality, but the industry's growth demographic was female, not male.

"Marianne, I'm so tired of penis," she'd said, some weeks back. "It's like how people at jobs get tired of certain things. Like how someone would say to their co-worker, 'I'm tired of batching reports.' Penis is like batching reports, Marianne."

But there'd been no definitive answer.

She headed toward the river, away from 5th Street. A wind came and lifted a burrito wrapper off the ground, the piece of foil scraping as it moved along the dry gutter. She reached the mouth of the alley and took the Alameda south, toward 6th Street and the Hotel Babylon and the long row of boarded-up storefronts. Scaffolding spanned the sidewalk; she walked in the street. A gunshot snapped off somewhere far away. No cars passed by. Tan weeds sifted in the wind in a fenced-off empty lot just beside her. She walked two more blocks, crossing on red, then turned the corner onto 6th, passing through the corner store's narrow entrance.

At the counter, buying a slim pack of mint-flavored gum, was Lindsay.

She put her head down and walked to the back of the store. She could tell the girl was following her with her eyes as she did it. She stared at the sodas, a hand on her hip. She wasn't ready to see someone she was interested in and now her skin felt like it was sitting wrong on her bones. Her toes squirmed, inside her stockings. She waited to hear some sort of exchange take place, and when she heard footsteps instead, her stomach pushed up in her chest. Lindsay tapped her on the shoulder. She turned around.

"Hi," Lindsay said.

"Hi," she said back to her.

The girl was wearing a Nirvana tank top and plaid flannel skirt that had once been a button down shirt. Her dark blonde hair was pulled back in a ponytail. Lindsay's green eyes were narrow and turned down at their edges. Her nose was Roman, a long, wonderful thing. She had thin lips and a wide mouth and great teeth, teeth that were regularly and professionally cleaned, teeth that had once, she was sure, harbored braces.

She reached into the cooler and pulled out a soda she didn't want. "Can I buy you your gum?" she asked. "I have to buy smokes."

"That's okay," Lindsay said. "I like your hair, though. It turned out pretty well."

"Were you still at the party when I did it?" she asked.

"Oh, no, I mean, I helped you do it," said Lindsay.

"Oh," she told her. The clerk was staring at them. Some frantically happy banda song played in the background, on the clerk's radio. The singer keened on in Spanish about a lost love. She looked down at her mint ballet flats. There were chunks missing in the floor's squares of linoleum.

They walked to the counter. Lindsay plunked down a quarter and picked up her gum. She was wearing blue heels with green flowers appliquéd on them.

"What kind of cigarettes should I buy?" she asked.

"I don't know, what do you smoke?" Lindsay asked.

"I don't have a brand, it's not like that," she told her. She bent down and took out a twenty from her shoe, standing up and asking for two packs of menthols. Lindsay stood there while she got her change, then they walked out of the store together.

"You're up at the Getty for the summer, right?" she asked.

"Yeah," said Lindsay. "End of July. I don't think I have enough to stay out here until the fall semester starts."

"Where do you go?" she asked.

"AIC," Lindsay said.

"I went to Princeton," she said. Lindsay gave her a look like she was telling a lie.

"No, I really did. Just a semester—I didn't graduate."

"You dropped out?" Lindsay asked. The buttons of the shirt ran down the center of the front of the skirt—little white buttons on big red and black plaid. Lindsay's legs were long, slim and tan; she imagined her sitting outside the museum, on lunch, eating a carrot stick from a plastic bag filled with identical sticks of carrot.

"Yeah, but I had to. My dad needed the money." As she told Lindsay this, she realized that it was first time that she'd ever told it to anyone at all.

"That sucks," Lindsay said. "You didn't try to get loans?"

"No," she told Lindsay. "I just moved back to Los Angeles."

A few cars pushed by on 6th. The sidewalk fencing was endless—long lengths of chain link, green tarp spread over the front of them. She'd peeked past every one and there was nothing to see—some building half-built, some stone slab where a building, someday, would be. She liked it when the tarps snapped in the wind, that sharp sound like a whip, like something small exploding.

"Do you live around here?" she asked.

"No," Lindsay said. "I was coming back from a friend's. I'm staying in West Hollywood. There's four of us in this studio. We don't have a fridge. This one dude sleeps on a hammock."

"Come live with me," she said.

"How much is rent?" Lindsay asked.

She curled her fingers up then touched her thumb to them.

"It's free," Lindsay said.

"It's gratis," she told her.

"You don't mean live in your room, though, right?"

"No," she said, though she hoped that she would. The air felt warmer than it had before.

"Can I think about it?" Lindsay asked.

"Sure," she said. "Do you want to come over? I'm getting interviewed soon—some German dude. It's this magazine out of London."

"What are they interviewing you for?"

"For my art," she said.

"For your movies?" Lindsay asked.

"No," she told her. "For my paintings. I do multimedia, too."

"I saw your billboard," Lindsay said. "That one by Bob Hope? I was picking my parents up at the airport. My older brother plays football for USC. He doesn't start or anything, though."

"That's cool, I guess," she said. She wrapped one of her arms over the front of her stomach.

"Yeah, it's one of the reasons that I took the thing at the Getty," Lindsay said. "He lives so far away now and like, never comes home. He didn't even come home for Christmas. He's really just on the team as a business connection. He's going to go get his MBA when he's done. He wants to be an investor for NFL players. Do you like football at all?"

"Do you want my number?" she asked. "You can call me if you want to come by."

"Sure," Lindsay said. "I'll put you in my phone. Um, I'm really sorry, but I forgot your name. I mean, I remember it, but I don't."

"Aubrey," she said.

"No, I mean your screen name. Your movie name," said Lindsay.

"Oh," she said. She told it to her.

"Cool," Lindsay said. "I knew the last name was a color, but I kept thinking green."

"Uh-uh," she told her.

"Can I get a picture with you, too? Here, hang on," Lindsay said, and took out her phone from one of her skirt's pockets, punching at the phone's screen with a finger. "Okay," she said. "Is this cool? Am I being lame?"

She touched at her bangs while she tried to smile, stepping toward Lindsay then turning around as the girl held her cell phone out in front of them. Lindsay put her arm around her. Her hand touched her neck. She realized that this was the first and last time this would happen. The flash went off on the phone.

"Awesome," said Lindsay. "Thanks." She took her arm off her. Lindsay asked for her number again and she told it to her.

"Did you really help me do my hair?" she asked.

"Yeah," Lindsay said, then let out a small laugh. "You were pretty fucked up. It was like five in the morning. I kept having to stop so you could go do more coke."

"Sorry," she said. A car drove toward her and she lowered her eyes, Lindsay turning to shadow, backlit by headlights.

"It's cool," she said. "I had fun. I was just happy my car was still there. Thanks for getting those bouncer guys to walk me."

"Sure," she said. "It's an unpredictable neighborhood."

"Do you want a ride?" Lindsay asked. She pointed at a black Jetta parked at the curb.

"It's okay," she said. "Call me if you want. The rooms go pretty fast, but I'd keep one for you."

"Cool," Lindsay said quickly, then walked around the front of the car, opening the door and waving before she got in. The Jetta's engine turned on and Lindsay pulled out. At the light, a block up, Lindsay turned around. Her heart began to beat faster in her chest, then slowed backed down after the girl kept driving by her.

She walked back to the warehouse, seeing no one at all. The alley off 5th Street was lined with bright tents. Sometimes she forgot that these tents housed people. She looked back behind her when she reached the fencing, putting the combination into the lock then sliding the fence back and shutting it behind her. She walked past the door that led up the stairs, walked past the parked cars that belonged to Monique and some of her friends whom she let park here. On the lot's far side was a thick iron door. The warehouse's mailbox was on the other side of it. She reached inside the cup of her bra and took out the key, swinging the alley door open and then turning her body around the corner of the building. She slid the key in the lock and opened the big steel mailbox door. She hadn't checked her mail for nearly a week; there were perhaps 200 letters. Lots of it was junk mail for roommates long gone: credit cards, home loans, auto insurance. She swept it all out from the mailbox at once, the pile smelling like lavender. Monique's mom perfumed her letters with this scent. Monique was from Kansas City. She had HIV. A year ago, a male actor had been hit by a car, and lost too much blood, and received a transfusion. This man had been with Monique in a scene the following month, for a series called *Forever Internal*. The news broke and Monique tried to die; she came home to Monique in her car, asleep and with all the windows up, a hose running from the muffler and then through her trunk, a folded up note next to her peppermint latte. She'd undone Monique's seatbelt and yanked her out. She knew Monique was breathing before Monique did, and this made her feel powerful in a cinematic way, like she was the holder of some special secret.

Upstairs, she threw the mail down on the couch, a seven-foot, red, real leather piece that had round copper bolts running up its arms and over its backing. There were two manila envelopes addressed to Artemis Blue. She knew what was in them. She ripped open one of the envelopes, the cards spilling out. Her agent handled all of her fan mail. Marianne then forwarded it on to her. She threw out anything that looked like it harbored stains. The rest she took with her into her bedroom, turning the light on at her drafting table. On the sill of the table she opened a small jar of blue paint, then a second jar of bright red, then a third jar of yellow. She opened the first letter, smoothing the folded paper out. This one was from Billy. Billy lived in Sonora. She had a small brush for each color of paint. She picked all three up and went into the bathroom, wetting their tips in the sink, then patting them dry with a hand towel. She went back to the bedroom and read the letter out loud, then made the appropriate corrections:

Hey Artemis,

You're so _____ing hot. I just caught you in your last Sinnmister Film, College Aged Devils #8. I love your small _____. Big _____are way overrated. Your _____ is perfect; the way you _____ that one dude, I couldn't stop staring at your _____ moving up and down. I stroked my _____ like five times to that scene. And the way that you played with his _____ while you looked right at the camera was so _____ing sexy. I have all your movies. I mean, I pay for them. I order them right from Sinnmister's website. I have _____ Queens of Mars and Artemis Does Michael and Artemis Does Ollie. That one scene from Teen Newbies like six years ago was one of the first _____ scenes that I ever watched. It was that one where your hair was dyed like really light blue and you took all of that dude in your _____? That was so _____ing awesome.

Anyhow, I just wanted to say I'm a big fan, and that you're like a goddess to me. I teach high school Science, Billy's not really my name, and I was saving up to come see you at AVN in Las Vegas, but I lost my job and don't have the money to make it. Hope to see you sometime soon, though! No one _____ _____ better than you! I love you!

Love,

Billy

She watched the paint glisten as it hardened and dried; she used different colors for different words—she'd done hundreds of these, perhaps one thousand. She picked the paper up and set it gently on her bed, then opened the next envelope, reading the letter. After twenty minutes, she got bored and stopped. She checked her cell phone. She had eighteen new messages. There was a party tonight at the beach, Monique said. There was a party tonight in the hills, Golem told her. There were parties tonight and there always would be, parties in Long Beach and Compton and Watts, parties in Bel Air and Studio City. People would drink and get drunk and eat food, and talk to one another about things that they liked and things that they didn't, politics, sports, some new fusion place, an annual report, an old carburetor. They'd speak of these things in tones quiet or loud; they'd raise their eyebrows and point with their fingers, before getting their coats and then saying goodnight and driving home to their house, to their apartment, to their trailer, and once they got there and the kids were tucked in or the trash taken out and the place was locked up and they were secure and alone and all cozy, thousands of people, the whole world around, would stare at some image of her short face, her long body. This image of her would twist, bend and bounce; she'd coo, scream and shriek in between moaning, and the rest of the world would just fall way for all of these watchers, these women and men, these teenaged boys, these priests and these teachers and coaches. They'd stare at her thighs, at her crotch, at her ass. They'd stare at some past version of her, some finite point on time's endless line, the rest of the world still moving ahead while they sat, transfixed, one point in space, watching another point in space that had already happened.

She took the brushes to the kitchen, washing them out in the sink, then filling up a champagne flute with water and setting the brushes inside the glass. She thought about the call from her dad, while she was at Princeton—*you have to come home, we ran out of money.* Those were his words to her, arriving from three times zones away while she pored over notes for her Life Science final. Her parents were lawyers, very rich, never there. Both hugged her and kissed her through money and things. She hadn't not liked it.

"Are you okay?" she'd asked.

"We are," her dad had said. "Book your flight. Use the credit card I gave you." Her father had been a lawyer for an NFL team. At sixteen, she'd had sex with one of the team's star players. From her New Jersey dorm room, she'd understood: the team had found out and her dad had been fired.

She'd flown home after finals with all her things. Her father had picked her up at the airport. He'd pulled up at Arrivals in his black Aston Martin. On the drive back, people stared and tooted their horns, the car just that cool, that much of a classic.

"It's because of him, right? The owner found out?"

They were stopped at a stoplight near the 405. Her father stared sternly ahead. Her mother handled estates and was out of country.

"I've found other work. We'll be fine," he'd said.

"So it's not about money," she'd said. "You're just punishing me."

"We'll be fine," her father repeated.

And she'd done it. It was more amazing now to her than it had been, then—the lie easier to go along with in the past than the present. She'd told her friends she just needed a break, the school too far away, etcetera, etcetera. Her parents moved to Chicago later that year. Neither of them spoke to her any longer. Her mom had left a voicemail, after they'd found out—*call us when you stop doing porn, and we might again let you be our daughter.*

She went back to the couch, taking the plastic wrapping off one of her packages of menthols. On the floor, by the arm of the sofa, she found a half-used book of matches. She lit her cigarette and shook the match out, throwing it on the table. She texted the journalist again—*when you are outside, have the taxi honk, and i'll come down and meet you.* She set the phone down. Another memory came back from the party—Dannell had asked if it was okay to put in the movie that showed on the screen. She remembered being on her bed, with Lindsay and Monique, her Sesame Street comforter bunched up around them, and Dannell coming in, in his boa and suit, and asking *please, Artemis, pleeeease, can't I show the movie.* She must have said yes—she remembered saying yes. She'd broken her own rule and now Dannell was gone forever.

The journalist texted back, just one word, *okay.* She got up from the sofa and walked back to her room, looking in her closet, at all of her clothes. The company that had put her face on billboards had also given her carte blanche to their entire catalog, for now and forever. She fingered a red bra on top of her chest of drawers; she touched at a turquoise foil print micromini. She stood there, in the strange shadows of her room, the bright light of her drafting table on one side, the darkness of her very big bed on the other.

The interviewer was short and had a mustache and a goatee, one of those things that ringed his mouth and chin and ironically made him look childish. She'd gotten his name wrong. His name was Sig. She didn't like how he looked. She thought he looked phony. He had on a blazer of black and tan tweed, a black collared shirt and black jeans and white sneakers. She was almost six feet and he was maybe five-four and as he got out of the backseat of the cab, and she walked up to him, this height difference brought up a silence after their initial helloes. She led him inside, up the narrow white staircase covered in years of graffiti. A severed unicorn's head was on the wall next to a Norteño 14, which was next to a peace sign, a drawing of an amp, a large swirl of stars in blue and red and grass green. From behind her, she heard the interviewer open his messenger bag, its Velcro tearing.

"Can I document this?" Sig asked. His accent was slight. She stopped walking and then turned around.

"Do whatever you want," she told him. She thought she'd been looking forward to the interview, but now that the German was here, she felt anxious. She should have begged off and gone out to the beach. It had been a long time since she'd been to the ocean, and she thought of the water, its lazy wrecked black, the moon overhead while the waves rolled and sifted. It sounded much better than sitting on the couch with a stranger. The German took out his Nikon and steadied himself on the stairs. She smiled a small smile while he snapped off his shots, walking up to the living room and sitting down on the red leather sofa.

Sig reached the main floor and looked around for somewhere to sit.

"We're furniture-impaired," she said. "I can sit on the floor, if you want the whole thing or something."

The German looked at her. "You've changed your hair," he said.

"From when to when? I change it a lot."

"On the billboards," he said, "your hair is black. You don't want people to know that that's you, or you would have kept your hair like it is in those pictures."

"That was last winter," she said. "That was six months ago."

"Still," he told her.

He cleared his throat and sat down on the edge of the couch. She'd taken a bright red saucer from the kitchen to use as an ashtray. From his messenger bag, the journalist brought out a handheld audio recorder. It was silver and looked very old. He gave her a forced smile, a sad, ugly thing, the sort of smile some clients gave her in hotel rooms, when she went to Miami. All of her porn she did in LA; for her escort trips, she flew to Florida. She did this once every couple of months, staying a week, charging five grand an hour. She posted the dates for these trips on her website. All of the slots filled up in the first twenty minutes.

She took a drag off her cigarette, held it, breathed out. She'd been sitting hunched over, her knees pressed together, and now leaned back on the sofa, crossing one leg over the other. She'd been five-eleven by the eighth grade. She was the tallest person in her class, and at her parent's urgings had tried out for the basketball team, becoming their starting center. She wasn't klutzy but also didn't care. She always passed when the ball came to her, her coach screaming at her from the sidelines to shoot it.

The interviewer set up his recorder on the table in front of the couch. He took out a small yellow notepad from a pocket inside the black messenger bag.

"Are you ready to start?" he asked.

"Sure," she said. She was horribly bored. There was cocaine in her room, in an amber candy dish that had once belonged to her grandparents. She wondered if she could excuse herself, put some up her nose. She imagined if she did this, though, that he'd know what she'd done, and then write about it. She put the cigarette out on the saucer. From past the window came the sound of a Dumpster lid slamming.

"So the subject for our first issue is art," the German said.

"Art isn't really a subject," she told him.

"You don't think so?" he asked, staring at her. They sat there a moment, neither saying a word.

"How many films do you think you've done?" the German asked her.

"One hundred and sixteen adult films," she said. "Three thrillers and one sci-fi movie."

"And those were speaking roles, in the thrillers?" the journalist asked.

"They were," she told him. "A few lines. Have you seen them?"

The German made a low humming sound, then shook his head. He lifted the hem of the leg of his jeans, scratching the skin of his calf with his pencil. He was wearing bright orange ankle socks. They didn't make sense. She liked their color.

"*Alien Landing* went straight to video, yes?"

"It did," she said.

"And you wanted more from it, I'm guessing."

"To my understanding," she said, "the director was promised a lot more money by the parent company financing the film. But that money didn't come through, and so we didn't have the budget for effects and the sets that we thought we would."

"Do you have a favorite set? From any of your films? Is there a certain landscape that stands out to you?"

"I was in this one film for Lurid? *Spikers*? It's the one about the volleyball team that's all vampires?"

The German nodded. "I know it," he said.

"You've seen it," she said.

"I know it," he told her.

She smiled at him. "So there's the orgy at the end? That rotating bed? I liked the red sheets and the blood on the walls. It didn't feel like fantasy. It felt like fantasy gone wrong. It felt like commentary."

"Are those your paintings?" the journalist asked.

She stared at them. "No," she lied. "They're someone else's."

The journalist looked at her like Lindsay had in the store, when she'd told the girl that she'd gone to Princeton.

"I'm going to turn the recorder on," Sig said.

"I thought it was on already," she told him.

The German punched a button. "Artemis Blue," he said. He smiled at her again. She didn't smile back.

"Is that your art on the wall?" the German asked.

"You already asked me that," she told him. She looked at the paintings and then down at her feet.

The German shifted now, uncrossing his legs. "I was trying," he said, "to give you another chance to answer the question."

They talked for an hour. She smoked six cigarettes. He asked her about orgasms and disease. He asked her about bondage and certain directors. He didn't ask one single question about art. The man's phone rang and he answered it and then said okay. "Taxi," he said, holding the phone in the air, out on front of him. "He's already outside."

"I'll walk you down," she told him.

Outside, she turned the combination on the carport fence's lock, letting the interviewer out into the alley. He got in the taxi and the taxi drove off. She locked the gate up, feeling odd, feeling empty.

Upstairs, she took out her laptop from her closet's floor and lay down on the bed with it. She typed "football hall of fame" into her search engine. She clicked on his name then clicked on his picture. It was from his heyday. They'd been at the owner's house, 4th of July. Her parents were there, along with five-dozen players, their children, their wives. He'd told her that he had something for her, upstairs. She'd met him before. He'd given her lots of attention. He'd been at their Christmas party, later that year, and it happened there, too, happened again in her own bedroom. The player had been benched and then traded away during her only semester at Princeton. After she'd been pulled from school and moved home, then moved out, and gotten her job serving drinks at the bar where she'd first met some industry stars, she'd taken a sick day and flown to Miami, the player she'd had sex with now retired to a villa next to an artificial lake. She'd waited for him in her rented car, near the gates at the end of his very long driveway. He hadn't seen her in nearly four years, but when she got out while he punched in the gate's code, he'd turned his bright green Mustang off and sat there, waiting. He didn't smile at her when she'd reached the car.

"How much do you want?" he said.

"Five grand a month for a decade," she answered.

"Three grand for eight," he said.

"Four," she said back.

"Four," he told her, then stuck out his hand, as though she were going to actually shake it.

"Cashiers' checks," she'd said, then handed him a piece of paper with her address. "The last week of the month." He'd only nodded. She'd never seen him again. She'd sent him a letter with her new address after she'd moved into the warehouse. He'd never once missed a payment.

In the pile of mail that had arrived over the week, along with her fan letters and the card for Monique, was the last check that he was obligated to send her. For eight years, and on the memo line of each check, was the date they'd agreed to terminate payments. The date had always seemed like a means to an end, a sad bit of revenge, recourse that worked partially and poorly. It hadn't ever felt like something that would arrive. Now, though, it had. It was a conclusion to a part of her life, but it also wasn't.

She logged into her website, checked the pictures, the number of hits. Some guy in the Valley that Marianne contracted maintained it for her. All that this man wanted in return were pairs of her underwear. She wondered what percentage of mail were things like this—secret tradeoffs, cashed vows of silence. She got off the bed and walked to her dresser, taking the tinfoil off the top of the candy dish holding the cocaine. On her drafting table's sill was the shell of a pen, the little man with a ball for a head waving at her. She picked it up and walked back to her dresser, lifting some coke from the dish with her finger, then dumping the powder on the dresser's wood top. She didn't sculpt it to lines; she just bent down and snorted. She set the pen down and then closed her eyes, waiting to feel it in the back of her throat. When she did, she coughed twice, holding it on her tongue and walking into the kitchen. She spat in the sink then turned on the faucet, finding a glass in the long row of cupboards. She rinsed her mouth out, her nose going numb. She wanted a cigarette and sand under her feet. She texted Monique—*are you still in Venice?*

When she got there, they were under the pier. The tide had gone out. She parked Monique's car on Abbot Kinney, next to a palm tree. A rip had begun in her left leg's thigh high. The lights from the walk didn't reach to the shore, but she could see their outlines, moonlit and very near to the water, fifty people at least, the glow of their cigarettes, their cell phones. She crossed the bike trail and walked onto the beach, stopping to sit down and take off her ballet flats and stockings. Her feet were damp and the sand clung to them. She liked the feeling. The pier went out a half-mile past the shore. She heard Monique's laugh, a deep perfect thing. A blue cooler of beer sat by one of the dock's tagged-up pilings. People looked at her as she bent down and took one. She'd worked with some of them and others she'd met—they were younger than her, late teens, early twenties. They came from Oklahoma, from Houston, from Tallahassee. They were like the palm trees that lined every drive—not native to here, fake but so fitting. She stared at their slim, bangled wrists. She looked at their feet; some were in heels, and she wondered if they'd worn them all the way out here, kept on their stilettos as they trudged over the sand. She touched at her hair. It hit at her chin. A few strands of white swung into her vision. She pushed them back. She'd forgotten that she'd dyed her hair to white, or that Lindsay had. She smoothed at it again while she looked around her.

She set down her shoes, stuffing her stockings inside them. Somehow she could barely hear the water, the waves—it was like the ocean, in LA, didn't work correctly. The fog hung in the sky. She touched at the wood on one of the pilings. People were gathered into fours and fives, talking about TV shows and hot rock massage and asshole bleaching. Monique walked up to her, out of one of these groups.

"My baby," Monique said. They hugged. "How are you?"

"I'm fine," she said. "I think that I might get my nose ring back in."

"Do it, girl. Everyone's grunge now. Or again or whatever."

She thought about Lindsay's skirt, the red and black flannel plaid. The little white buttons that ran down its center. The last lover she'd taken was two years ago, a guy at a bar that she'd met at the yearly Vegas convention. After the signing, after the flashing of tits, after business cards given out by men wanting and hoping, she'd gone to her room in a tower at Caesar's. She'd pulled on black jeans and a plain black t-shirt and put on her shades and gone down for a drink at a bar tucked away in one corner of the casino. It had taken ten minutes for a fan to spot her. She'd been stirring her Mai Tai and he'd sat down on a stool.

"I'll leave right now if this isn't okay," he'd said.

"People always say that exact thing," she'd told him.

He lived outside Vegas and they drove north in his car, away from the city and out into nothing. When she did things like this, she questioned if she wanted to die, if some mute part of her, very deep down, hoped to and needed to perpetually be in situations in which she might get in trouble. If she sabotaged herself unknowingly, scared of success, and in doing so subverted her own potential.

The man lived by himself fifty miles out of town in a six-bedroom mansion in the middle of the desert. They talked about films, both porn and mainstream. They talked about fashion and mystery novels. He owned three cats and a boa constrictor. Behind his house was a firing range; he'd grown up in LA and celebrities would come out and shoot off his guns. His family was rich, his father a TV director.

"You aren't lonely out here?" she'd asked. They'd been in his basement, surrounded by rifles. The walls were red velvet, the carpet bright black. The room's chandeliers were made from deer skulls and antlers. He'd shrugged after she'd asked him her question.

"I like being lonely, I guess," he'd said.

"But you aren't sure," she'd said.

"No, I guess not," he'd said.

"Yeah," she'd said. "Me either."

They'd gone out to his backyard and shot off AKs then come back inside and had sex on his couch and she'd spent the night there. The next day, he'd driven her back into town; he owned an old truck, a black antique Chevy.

"I'd like it if you called me the next time you come in," he'd said, when they'd reached the underground drop-off at Caesar's.

"Okay," she'd told him, but then never did, and didn't really know why, and this not knowing why, on occasion, made her flustered.

Monique was wearing an emerald ball gown. A slit ran up its side to the jut of her thigh, her brown skin almost black, her thigh smooth and gorgeous. She had on drop earrings. Their gold chains dangled down. She had a weave in, strands of pink and dark blonde, a wide black hair band keeping it off her face.

"Did that journalist show up? I stayed away," Monique said.

She took a sip of her beer. "Yeah, but it was dumb. I've got a letter from your mom in the car."

"Shit, I've got to get one of those change of address things," Monique told her.

She remembered now—Monique was moving away. She was moving back home, or almost was, was leaving LA for life in the Midwest. Monique had a bottle of rum in one hand and a can of lemon-lime soda in the other. Her toenails were painted a very bright red.

"Monique, I don't want you to leave, though," she told her.

Monique made a sad sound and set her drinks down in the sand, then leaned in and hugged her. "My mom hasn't seen me in eight years," Monique said. Monique kissed her on the cheek, then picked her drinks back up off the sand.

"You're fine," Monique said. "You're the queen of LA."

"I'm the queen of LA," she repeated.

They talked a while longer about a new tapas place, about a stray dog that Monique saw get hit by a car, about which actors were secretly fucking which celebrities. The beer had warmed up some and she poured it out on the sand, the liquid raising up into a white foaming mass.

"Are you going to escort, when you move back?" she asked.

"Aubs, I got in to law school at UMKC," Monique said. "I told you this months ago. You really have to start remembering things better."

"I'm sorry," she said. "Did we have a big party?"

"We did," said Monique. "You pulled that girl's hair and she blew out her knee. She's contract now, you know, over at Lurid."

She tried to think back. She was still staring at the puddle of foam. She remembered making a volcano in the fifth grade, the tissue-wrapped baking soda dropped in, the fake lava spilling out, spilling over. She'd constructed the volcano from papier-mâché, sat by herself at the dining room table. Her mom had come home as the lava frothed out. *What are you doing,* her mother had screamed. *What are you getting all over my table?*

"Can I take your car up to the Hills?" she said. "Golem's up there, at some other party."

"You totally like him," Monique said, pointing at her. "Admit it. You like muscleheads."

"No I don't," she said, and they both started laughing. The moon was a little tear past the fog. She hugged Monique again and turned to leave, setting her beer bottle down and picking up her shoes and stockings. She was halfway to the car when someone ran up behind her, tapping her three quick times on the bone of her shoulder. She turned around. The guy was Latino and looked in his teens. His hair was slathered with gel and dyed blonde, the tips of it standing up like the tines on a fork. He had on grey sneakers and dark blue girls' jeggings. His t-shirt was skintight and the same pale yellow as her dress. The front said VALLEY APPLIANCE in red curly letters.

"Is that Mystique?" the boy said, motioning back down the beach. Mystique was Monique's screen name. She didn't work anymore but still had a fan base. The boy was holding a joint in one hand and had on a stuffed animal backpack, an all-white gorilla that scared her.

"Why?" she'd said back, though she should have said no, and immediately regretted not saying it.

"She's got it, right?" the boy said.

"Got what?" she said back.

"The bug," he said. "She's got HIV, right?" he asked her.

"I don't know what you're talking about," she said, and started walking away from him, back toward the car.

"Wait," the boy said, "wait, wait a second."

She was walking very fast but he ran and caught up with her. She stopped. She looked back down toward the water. Monique was facing away from her, talking with a cameraman that they knew. The boy swung the gorilla backpack around in front of him. Its zipper ran from one ear to the other. He pulled out a baggie filled halfway with pills. She stared at the bag. There were seventy-five in there, one hundred.

"You're Artemis Blue, right?" he asked.

"Maybe," she told him.

"Here, take them," the boy said. "They're cat valium. Pure Special K. My dad's a vet. They're good, I promise."

"Why do you want to give them to me?" she asked.

"Introduce me," he said. "Introduce me to Mystique. I want what she's got. I'm a bug chaser," he said. "I think she's gorgeous."

He stood there expectantly, like he'd said something proud. She could see his dark nipples through the thin yellow shirt. She looked back down the beach, toward the pier, scanning the party for bouncers, for muscle.

"Hang on a second," she told the boy. "You stay right here." She took the bag from him and started walking back toward her car.

"Wait, where are you going?" the boy called from behind her.

"My cell isn't with me," she said. "I'm parked right up there. I'm going to go get it and take a picture of you, and if she likes what she sees, I'll introduce you."

"Do you think she will?" the boy asked. The backpack's straps were the gorilla's long arms.

"I do," she said. "Just wait a second."

She got back to the street and unlocked the car. Her cell was sitting next to the letter from Monique's mother. She texted Monique—*is there muscle down there.*

Monique texted back—*two guys, you okay?*

She texted back—*yellow shirt, up toward the street, bug chaser, wants you, have someone get him.*

Monique texted *okay* and she sat there in the car, watched a huge white guy in all black she'd not seen before walk out of the piling's long shadows and toward the boy. She started the car and pulled out from the curb, the pills in her lap, the palm trees all around her.

She took Venice to Western and headed north to the Hills. It took her a long time to find the address. She parked on the shoulder and climbed over the gate, touching it once to make sure that it wasn't electric. The driveway was sandstone and went down and down. Ahead of her, the door to the house was open. Something made her sure that she'd been here before. She paused at the threshold and then stepped inside. The wide foyer led to a sunken living room where a trio of girls danced on a portable stage that had chrome poles that ran up toward the ceiling. There were TVs mounted along three of the walls. A pop song played loudly. The women writhed, topless and horribly bored. Three men sitting very close together watched them from a sofa. There was a deck past the living room, a group standing out there. A man came out of a swinging door to her right. Past him, she could see a gas stove, a row of copper pots hanging above it. The man was holding a plate of miniature soufflés. The food smelled of some type of cheese and green onion. The man had a spray tan, expensive-looking eyeglasses. His black hair was made up in a messy fauxhawk, the bangs pulled to one side, the top and the back shaggily pointed. He had on a black sport coat and a white shirt and black tie. She moved to take a soufflé and the man pulled the plate back from her.

"No dancing on a full stomach," he said. "We don't want you to cramp. It's like swimming, yes? Do you need a bathroom to change in?"

She stared at him. She was holding the bag of pills in her hand. "I'm not here to dance. Where's Golem?" she asked. There was something in the kitchen she knew.

"What's Golem?" the man said.

"The security," she said. "Big guy. He probably came with the dancers."

The man waved his free hand. It bent back at the wrist. "Oh, that guy," he said. "That guy is so gone. I thought he was going to punch one of the guests for touching your cohorts."

"They're not my cohorts. I don't know them," she said. She realized the man was wearing a half-apron.

"Oh my god," he said. His eyes went big. She was still thinking about the kitchen. "Oh my god," the man said again. "You're Artemis Blue. I didn't realize it because of the hair."

"Uh-uh," she told him. "I don't know who that is." A stripper with a black ponytail and elegant nose and big blue eyes turned her head to one side and put up her arms as she slithered. The men's mouths were flat: no smiles, no frowns. One of the men couldn't stop blinking. All three held red plastic cups in their hands. It was the floor, the kitchen floor, she thought. She had been here before. She was nearly sure of it.

"Who owned this house, before you?" she asked. The man was smiling insanely at her. She was trying, in her mind, to remove him from the space, to rewind her life so that she could remember.

"I have no idea. A family," he said. "But come on, you're Artemis Blue, right? You can tell me the truth. We won't tell anybody." The man set down the soufflé tray on the foyer's white rug. "Look, I have no idea how you wound up here," the man said, "and I don't want to come off like a freak, but I am really, really hoping you'll stay. You have no idea what big fans we are. Everyone here. Seriously, everybody. We were just talking about you like an hour before. I know how that sounds, but you have to believe me."

She was still thinking about the green floor. There were little square tiles, ceramic, the color of jade. She remembered touching at them before she plunged in the needle. She was looking at them and then she was a bright, wet thing, and then her vision went black and she woke up in a night-gown, in a hospital. Was that right? Was this that house? It was up in the Hills, a guy from high school. He'd gone on to open a coffee plantation in Belize. He'd been home for Christmas, his parents out of the country. She was just back from Princeton, for then and forever. Someone at her work had given her the bag. She'd had it for weeks and then Christmas arrived and the guy texted her, listing off names of celebrities who would be in attendance. She'd shot up with the agent of one of these stars. Was this that house? She was holding the pills. The music was so loud, the pop singer's voice auto-tuned, overdubbed in quintuple.

"Do you want all of these?" she asked the man, holding the bag of cat Valium out at him. "I'll give them to you if I can go in your kitchen."

"Look," the man said, "just hang on a second. Steven!" the man yelled. He was trying to get the attention of the men on the couch. "Do whatever you want," he said. "Just stay here a second."

She nodded while the man walked down the stairs to the living room. Out on the deck, through its glass doors, people were staring at her. One of them started to come in from outside. She put her head down and walked into the kitchen. Alone with the ovens and islands and rows of pots, she realized the room wasn't where she'd shot up. She had been here, but it was much longer ago—an errand run with one of her au pairs when she was maybe ten or eleven. The au pair was Spanish; the home's owner was, too. The au pair and the man had gone off to another part of the house, and she had waited in this kitchen, touching at things, opening the refrigerator and taking out a half-finished bottle of white wine and removing the cork and sniffing at the liquid inside. The au pair came back as she was shutting the door. The bun of her hair was pushed to one side.

"Your lipstick's messed up," she'd told the woman.

The man in the apron came into the room, followed by the three men from the couch.

"Holy shit, no way," one of them said. A fifth man pushed into the kitchen.

"Okay," the man in the apron said. "We got it ready. I can't believe this. I just can't believe this."

He was panicked with excitement. She realized that the music had stopped. The five men were standing there, staring at her. It was out of such staring that she had food to eat, that she had a property that she owned, had coke for her nose, a contract for clothing. It wouldn't be like this much longer, she knew. She worked in an industry not known for employee longevity. The man swung his hand, beckoning her. She did what he asked, setting the bag of pills on the counter. She walked past the white door, looked out at the room. The dancers stood next to the poles, putting on their clothes. All of the TVs had gone black. Everyone from the deck had come inside.

"We skipped the opening credits," the man in the apron said. "We wanted to get right to the opening scene." He was smiling. His skin was nearly pumpkin, nearly Halloween. One of the men who had come into the kitchen was holding a remote controller.

"Are you ready?" the man holding the remote asked.

"I don't know," she said.

He pressed a button and the movie came on. The screen version of her was sitting in a uniform in a spaceship's captain's seat.

"Captain, the force fields are down," a character said to her character.

She was looking at the people, looking at her on the screen. A woman was sitting on the arm of a couch and their eyes met and the woman smiled and then pushed back her hair and looked down and then looked at her again, before looking back at the TV. She could feel herself blushing. She touched her hair, too.

"Captain," the actor said. "What do you want to do?"

Past the deck, in the distance, was all of LA. She was mouthing along, without intending to, speaking words that she'd already spoken.

Lost Cultures of the Ancient World

He's walking. It's nighttime. It's summer, late June, no thrum of cicadas, no whine from a train, just damp windless air and bright stars overhead as he descends his porch steps of wrecked brick and chipped mortar, the foundation of the house leaning south out of age and decay, the living room walls pulling apart at their corners, the house trying to grow, to uproot and leave, to abandon its form and its math and its makers, to be something past refuge, past safety or shelter, trying, he thinks, to become the impossible—a structureless structure—and the cobblestone pathway that leads to the street has been warped to bulbous by roots underneath, fans of weeds pushing through the path's rifts and fissures, and there was the time his ex-wife fell while holding a vase, caught her foot on a bump and pitched the vase forward, the glass vessel turning as it flew through the air and then broke to shards on the porch steps below him, his wife's elbow bruised, her knee bloodied, these acts things he'd watched from his spot in the doorway before going inside and finding the dustpan and whiskbroom—these acts over a year ago now, and while they took place here, on the porch steps he's just passed, they seem to him part of a separate age, part of a different era.

His shoes are black canvas with rubber soles. Splotches of paint dot the toecaps, the vamps. Eyelets are missing. The ends of the laces have frayed themselves thin and the insoles, from time, have ceded all bolster. He feels every step as he reaches the sidewalk, a red brick path perhaps ten inches wide that leads south to the road that he takes up to school and north, toward her old apartment. Across the street, to the east, is a big empty lot where decades ago, long before he ever heard of this town, three houses caught fire and burned to the ground, their roofs caving in, their walls blackened from smolder, the first structure collapsing onto the next and the second house in turn igniting the third, the destruction occurring on the cusp of July and August, the students all gone, the windows all darkened, the smoke twisting and snaking before turning thick. Now, though, trimmed grass, a trio of elms that survived through the heat and the fire trucks' hoses. The city could put in a sandbox and swings and the lot would look planned, seem empty on purpose. One society's doom, he's told class after class, is another's inception.

Past the trees is a bank; its bulbs backlight the lot. A feral cat stalks through the shadows, high-stepping. He's walking to meet her. She's come back to town. He hasn't seen her in over six weeks. Her texts have been vague, have been terse and half-hearted. But this morning a present: *the train tracks: can we meet?* She set a time and he told her he'd be there. This night is a night of hope and repair. He's wearing the bright red knee socks she likes. He's wearing frayed shorts that used to be khakis. His black t-shirt is threadbare, forty years old. Across its front, in gold, is the word FORGOTTONIA. Three pieces of paper, folded to thirds, sit in his left side pocket. This is a love letter, he will say at the tracks. This is a love letter for you, where you're from, for what you've been through and what's transpired between us. This is a love letter for each detail and kiss, for each night we stayed up to listen to storms, for each morning we woke entwined and naked. This is a love letter for the sweat in between, for the cigarettes. This is a love letter that just you will see since no one else ever could know of our love as it would have meant change we did not want to deal with. This is a love letter to all that we killed; this is a love letter to what died around us. He'll hand her the letter once he's read it in full. He'll look in her eyes and make her eyes brighten.

The stray cat scampers off into the night and then the lot and the elms are behind him, the grass growing up over the sidewalk, its bricks, the long blades padding his steps as he passes the house of his neighbor, an elderly bachelor with the last name of Smith who grew up in this town and has lived here all his life and bought and sold gun memorabilia. The house is light yellow with trim in dark plum. The copper shingles are scalloped and mint green from patina. A big pine's boughs droop between Smith's house and his own. The limbs scratched at his study's windows all winter, the ice-hided nettles a metal glove over glass. Their shrieks made him shiver, the tree leaning from squall. He'd wake before dawn and compile, doing research, his wife asleep in their bedroom across the short hall. His wife frowned in her sleep, her dreams disappointing. He'd grown up in a city overlooking the Pacific and hated that city whenever he was there, and missed it whenever he wasn't. His ex-wife is from Nebraska. The first summer he went to her parents' farm, he saw a pelican. He was standing in the dirt driveway, smoking a cigarette, when the fat, white bird flew over. It was August, almost sunset. At dinner, he told his wife's parents about seeing the bird. They looked at him with a dull, unimportant sort of wonder, the same way that with time he would look at his wife, and on that day looked at the pelican.

He reaches the corner and crosses the street, walking past the school that her brother once attended, the ten-room building a place for delinquents to learn while kept separate from students with a future ahead of them, kids who were not addicted to meth by fourteen, and selling it to a three-county customer base two years later. The front of the school has a long frescoed wall. Among bits of old tile and steel sit glass, the corner streetlight reflecting off these shards, showing parts of his shadow as he passes by it. To the right, the road climbs toward a trio of dorms and the building that houses Administration. The Provost told him the policy was firm: a relationship with a student was grounds for dismissal. But this night is a night of hope and repair. This night is a night in which he will pick up the pieces. Everything will work out. He knows that it will. They'll hire him back. His evals are stellar. He's published in journals. He's done good service work. She's three miles away and he'll see her soon. He hasn't seen her, it feels like, in ages.

He stops, turns around, walks back past the school—he's forgotten his cigarettes. He swings his thin body, spins on one foot, the collection of keys he keeps clipped to the loop of his shorts hitting him in the hip and then jiggling. In the past year he's taken off twenty pounds; he runs every day, lifts weights and does sit-ups, then goes back to the gym in the evening and swims, his muscles' movement in the blue of the pool more relaxing than a glassful of whiskey, a beverage that he hasn't had in over ten years and would not have again, not now and not ever. Across the street from the school stands an old battered house. Its porch holds bikes, five of them wound with the same curling chain around a rotting wood railing. A breeze blows and he looks down at his feet. Two autumns from now, he will turn forty. He's nearly forty years old and wearing knee socks. He's nearly forty years old and still smoking. He watches two bats circle a pair of big elms. As he steps into the street, a truck full of teenagers runs the stop sign. He pauses, waiting for them to pass by, reaching out a finger and touching one side of a taillight. The plastic is smooth. He can smell the exhaust. Two months ago, he sold his Explorer. He's been growing his hair out for over three months and has now shaved almost all of it off, save for a stripe down the middle of his head, which he dyed pink and then spiked. He hopes that she'll like it; she likes surprise. She likes the effort that surprise endeavors. He bought her gifts often: new panties, a bangle, a blouse. The gifts never impressed her, but their surprise did. When she told him this, his heart moved in quick little circles.

He looks past his house, down the block, to the north. The soil rises up in long, smooth humps in between all of the driveways. The first place he kissed her was on one of these patches of grass. They'd been at a student house known for its parties. An Irish kid from Chicago's South Side had invited him over—they were having a formal. He went under the guise of being a chaperone. He actually went because he knew she'd be there. The party was loud, everyone drunk, a group in the attic doing lines of cocaine in between games of ping-pong. He'd left with her after midnight and walked over toward school and two hours later they were on the rug covering his office floor, and then nothing else mattered. But now it's summer, the air without wind, the air damp but rainless. He turns on to the house's crumbling brick path and leaps up the stairs and onto his porch and then opens his front door and walks past it. His cigarettes are on the entryway table. He looks through the front room to the dining room, then the kitchen. All of the walls are painted sky blue, the color of the lawns of celestial beings—all the gods, all the gods, all their stories. The house's ground floor is bare, save for a table that harbors a large pile of bills. He can't pay them yet, but is sure he will soon. This night is a night of hope and repair, and there's one letter that's getting near to overdue, and in this letter's words he'll find his salvation. He goes back out the front door. Now he is ready. Now he's on his way. The breeze blows again. He can smell the rain in it.

Her name was Presley, an impossible name, a name that had conscribed her to an abnormal existence. Her mom had suggested the name and her dad had said yes, and her dad said yes to everything that he could, as it was his way of not responding. Her dad worked at the ball bearing plant on the east side of town. Her childhood backyard had harbored a barn with a fallen-in roof. She'd grown up milking goats, shooting rabbits. On the first day of the only class that she'd taken from him—Lost Cultures of the Ancient

World—she'd been wearing jean shorts, a flannel shirt tied off at the waist, and cowboy boots that she'd spray-painted bright green. She'd held his gaze when he'd looked at her, and he'd felt his life change, some nearly indiscernible shift that caused rumblings and echoes of rumblings.

He walks back past the school then keeps heading south, toward the train tracks and center of town, the latter no more than a courthouse and park and motley collection of closed shops and small churches. Ahead the road curves, after the tracks, the town cut to quarters by a pair of state highways. One of these runs north, up toward the Quad Cities, and south toward St. Louis and Presley. The other—the road he's looking at now—runs east–west, and harbors all of the box stores and restaurant franchises out near the town's edges. They've never been to any of them together, but he sometimes thinks of them there, pushing a cart down the Wal-Mart's wide aisles, dumb-eyed and touching at things, having small fights about sauce pans or area rugs: is the color just right, do they really need it.

Wrecked blocks of granite stand four feet high on a small patch of grass next to the roadside. At the street before the tracks he heads west, away from the university. He walks down a one-way that dips and then rises, the blocks' houses mismatched and weathered, most of their lights off, most of their porches leaning to one side, the earth below them shifting from rain and snow and heat, from the relentless march of the seasons. Realty signs lean over lawns of tall grass. Window screens peel away from their windows. Most of the mailboxes are full, their tinny insides stuffed with coupon books. He considers the process of how the books were made, how they were produced and then printed and shipped, and lugged in some pouch by some gruff mail carrier. The majority of societies failed, he's told class after class, because of improper use of resources. There was some lack of foresight, of looking ahead, and by the time that it came to cut back, the paucity in question had become too crippling to bear. The problem was that the society in question couldn't accept this. There was a lack of perception, of reasoned consequence—even if things were a little bad now, these societies assumed they would always get better. The future, for them, was dyed brightly with hope, and when this hope failed, these societies vanished.

The clouds roiled and did so just as clouds had over Akkad, over Sippar and Kish and old Babylonia. The clouds roiled as they had over the Hurrians and Mitanni, over Tuthmose III, over the Kasku Tribes and the Black Sea and Egypt. The clouds roiled as they had over the Savromat and Sarmat antiquities. The clouds roiled as they had over the pot-smoking Scythian nomads. The clouds roiled as they had over the great Petén Basin, over jaguars and tapir and toucans and agouti, over Calakmul and over Tikal, over the altars to Ah Muzencab, god of the bees, over the Serpent Head Polity's ball courts, their gore and their rock and their glory. The clouds shifted and swayed and built on themselves, grew and collapsed and moved very fast across the night skies and over the Pyramids and the Sphinx, over the Nazca lines in southern Peru, over the legendary lost world of Mu, over Tambora and over Atlantis and over the Spirit Mummy Cave thirteen miles east of Fallon, Nevada. The clouds roiled, disquiet, turbulently disturbed, huge bloated shapes of black and dark gray that held crests and edges before turning again, the wind bringing them east, the wind bringing them nearer.

He reaches the hill's top. The road levels out. To his left, to the south, are more darkened houses, more verdant elms, more bats flitting like wind-taken kites just under the canopy the elms' boughs created. Two blocks down is the state road, the small Dairy Queen. Through the autumn, before winter came, he and Presley went there once a week, one of them stay-ing hidden behind the tinted windows of his Explorer while the other went and bought sundaes or freezes. They'd drive south, toward Quincy, past quarries and fields, past long-closed gas stations and small lakes for fishing. She'd roll down her window, the breeze taking her hair, the long, coarse, blonde strands swaying and shaking. She owned two pairs of shoes—her green boots and red Keds. Depending on which of these she wore to class, he knew if she'd be able to meet him that night. The green boots meant she could; the red Keds meant she couldn't. When she came to class with the green boots on, his cheeks turned the red of the shoes that she wasn't wear-ing.

Tonight, at the shop, there's a line—it wraps around the worn, stone side of the building. The moon turns the sky blue over the street. Porch lights are on. Cars sit in driveways. He watches a trio of girls laugh under the shop's bright white lights, their legs very tan, their hair pulled back and banded. All three wear flip-flops and talk at each other while texting. A dog barks. A truck's fan belt whines. Next to the shop the light changes from red to green; the house across the street, which he thought pink, now looks the color of mint chip ice cream—Presley's favorite. He looks the other way, toward the clouds and the school, staring at the cupola on top of Shirley Hall, its gold-painted plaster. Above the main door is the Provost's large window, a half-circle designed to look like a transom. Glazing bars run through its glass like sunbeams, their lengths spanning out over the pane from one single point at the bottom, in the center.

His final for Lost Cultures of the Ancient World was one essay question—if you could live in any of the societies we studied, which would it be, and what would be your role in it? Presley answered a common citizen of Greece—*I'd like to be able to move through the streets without any preconceived notions of duty*. He copied this sentence down on paper with pen, taping the quote to the wall above his desk and computer.

He passes more houses, an ugly brick church. The trees fall away as he walks farther west, away from downtown, its courthouse and bars. The campus, a street over, comes to an end. He walks ten minutes more, smoking, not thinking at all. He reaches Prairie Avenue, the west end of town. Groups of cream-colored apartment buildings stand to his left; they buffer the sound from the state road just past them. In one of the windows, along the wall facing him, a light comes on inside an apartment. The building is set back from the street; he sees a girl appear, then the blue of a TV screen. On occasion, Presley would pose nude for him. They'd arrange times when he would drive by her house, which sat on the corner of a nearby block, and had a dirt alley that her bedroom's window looked out on. She'd text him and give him a time, and he'd tell his wife he was going out to get smokes, or if she was asleep, tell her nothing. He'd take the Explorer north, to the white two-level she shared with her roommate, take a right past the house then turn into the alley. She'd be standing in profile with her blonde hair trailing down and one arm akimbo. He'd drive by slowly, gravel crunching under his tires, her room's lamp set on the sill of the window, front-lighting her, and then he'd be past the house and back on the street, his heart beating fast, his limbs near to tingling.

A summer ago, they took a trip to Cahokia Mounds, after his wife had moved out forever. The trip was a weekend affair, he and Presley staying at a chain hotel and visiting the site for only an hour, before returning to the hotel room, its bed, and doing over again what they'd done that morning. The Mounds had no written records, just wood, copper and shell, shards of pottery that held broken symbols. He remembers little of the trip past the hotel room itself, a wide ray of sunlight getting in between the room's curtains as her body rose and fell. After, he told her about Elizabeth Báthory de Ecsed, the Hungarian countess and serial killer who was put on trial for the mutilation of young girls, torturing and killing, by some accounts, as many as 650. The most popular legend that grew out of these acts was that the Countess then bathed in the blood of her victims.

"The innocent," she said, and he said yes, then put his lips on her thigh, then his head, thinking again of the Mounds and the lives inside the life, the pottery shards that held fragments of symbols. His own life feels like this to him, too—sharp lengths of hard clay that meant something once, but too many of which could never be found, the vessel too damaged to be put back together.

But this night is a night of hope and repair. This night is different. A car turns from the state road, coming his way. He crosses while it's still a half-mile down, descending into the landscape and darkness. He knows this road well: the hill down, the hill up, then nothing but miles of flat land, save for the bluff that the trestle passed over. The wind smells of dirt. The foxtails bend away from him.

In the last twenty minutes, one car has passed by: a brown Buick driven by a very old man. The car's dome light was on. The man's hands clutched the wheel. The man looked like he will, when he's very old. The man hadn't seen him.

The air warms as clouds fill the sky. He wonders if there's going to be a tornado. Presley's dad liked to chase them in his old silver truck; he'd welded a Y-bar to the driver's side door, on which he'd mounted his video camera. A local news station, some years ago, used her dad's footage of an F-4 he'd caught. He'd tracked the twister as it had gone through a town and then taped its aftermath—all of its damage. National media paid for the clip, as did a pair of programs that spotlighted disasters. It was these sums that helped cover Presley's college tuition.

He puts his hand in his pocket, to get out a smoke. Something is missing that he knows should be there. He pats at his thighs, but it's gone, the note, the three folded-up pieces of paper. He stops walking, looks back in the direction he's come, the Buick's taillights red dots in the distance. The note fell out, he thinks, and it's lying back there, in a gutter somewhere, in a patch of foxtails. He keeps walking. There's no other choice. His Union Rep told him not to fight—just resign, she said, you can't beat this. They were downtown, at a café on the square, a few days after his initial suspension.

"History is full of impossible victories," he said.

"It isn't," she said. "We just highlight those few, but you know this. Her family's against you. Just walk away."

"I could talk to them," he said.

The union rep was digging through her bag. She stopped and looked him in the eye. "Who do you think," she asked, "told the school in the first place?"

But he's right—he's sure that he is. There was Gettysburg, Troy, the Battle of Rorke's Drift, the Reliefs of Lucknow and Hill 875 and D-Day. He'll win because he has to, because he can't lose, because losing translates to no reason to live, and he was living again for ten years, a decade of no booze, his anniversary just weeks ago, though he stopped going to meetings a long time before that, around the time that he started seeing Presley. Ten years of new life: she'd wanted him to explain what it was like, and he told her it's like I died but death didn't exist, like how gods die but then go on living.

He pulls his shirt away from his chest. Against the backs of his knees he can feel the strings hanging from the bottom of his shorts, the thin ragged lengths of tan fabric. He has eighty-six dollars in his checking account. His credit cards are maxed out. He's cut them up. July rent is a riddle he can't figure out, but the letter will come and say the right things and the bills will get paid and all will be better. He keeps walking west, a shelterbelt to his left, a long line of dark trees against the dark sky. Thunder cracks and then sifts and then cracks again, in the other direction. They've had a wet spring, the fields wrecked, the fields flooded. His knee socks have come down from over his calves. He touches at one side of his freshly shaved head, then at the line of hair down its middle. When he was young he read fantasy books and his favorite parts of those books, every time, was not the beginning or the inevitable battle, just before the end, but some scene in the middle that left the hero lost, alone on some cliff or the dune of a beach, languishing, a new sudden wanderer. He found those moments so gripping, when young, he'd wanted to put the book down and strike out on his own, pull on a sweatshirt and fill up a pack and find himself east, on the edge of some forest, where he would live off the land and sleep under the trees and much time would pass and he would grow up and grow stronger, then return to his homeland and right all those wrongs before being called off on some new adventure. In those tales' moments, the hero looked like he would lose, though this never turned out in the end to be true. If this were the case, he thinks now, picking his pace up as the rain starts to fall, the hero would be called something different.

He sees the black trestle, the road running beneath, the short bluff cut in half, the rusted steel girding. He doesn't know why the tracks run over the hill, as opposed to around them. Perhaps flash flood, he thinks. Perhaps sudden emergency. Perhaps he can find out who owns these tracks, ask how much it might cost to help with their upkeep. The first half of his life was about tearing things down; his life's second half can be about reconstruction. There's symmetry there, a balancing out. This night is a night of hope and repair. They weathered the world's brusque welcomes before and can do so again—he is sure of it. He'll patch things up with her brother once he's out of rehab, talk things through with both of her parents. He's already tried this with her Dad—walked into the ball bearing plant where he works, asked a foreman where he could find him. Who are you, the foreman asked, and he told him his name and the foreman said wait a minute. The foreman came back with three other men. Get of out of here, the foreman said. You're trespassing.

And this word—trespassing—when they drove northwest to the Iowa clinic, her breasts growing larger and feeling sore, her stomach, each morning, growing queasy. He sat in the waiting room with two other men, neither of them out of their twenties. The clinic's nurse, perched behind bulletproof glass, had asked his relation to her. "Friend," he said, the nurse holding his stare for just long enough to say *bullshit* with her eyes, without ever saying it. Behind her was a sign one could buy at a hardware store, the trim in all white and the background bright black and the words—NO TRESPASSING—in bright orange block letters. Presley elected to have the procedure offsite—a pill that she took, that shattered the fetus. They rented a hotel room five cities away, staying three nights in a fifth floor king suite. Each night, she slept on the bathroom floor. He listened to her vomit and cry. He smoothed her hair and said things he hoped would help her. He'd told his wife he was attending a conference one state away. The day he got back, she tripped up the stairs with the vase.

"Oops," his ex said. "Guess I did something wrong." She stared at him in the same way the clinic nurse had.

"That's okay," he said, staring back, then taking his wedding ring off and dropping it on to the floor of the porch, "from time to time, we all make poor decisions."

The rain has eroded his mohawk's gel; the long strands of dyed pink paint the crown of his skull like a comb-over. The bluff sits to the left of the road, the short span of asphalt that runs under the tracks one hundred yards in the distance. He thinks of her quote, taped to his wall—*I'd like to be able to move through the streets without any preconceived notions of duty.* Its paper has yellowed, the ink lightening some. The tape has dried out and he's had to replace it, but the words won't change, not now and not ever. They'll walk the banks of the Volga and the Seine, the Danube and the Thames and the Loire and the Dniester. They'll spend a whole summer doing nothing but walking by rivers. He'll take her parents with them, fly them overseas, save up for a few months and get a group rate and they can try crepes and gaze up at Big Ben and go look at where the Berlin Wall once stood, and now stood no longer. He'll show them that he can be good, that he can provide, that he isn't a quitter. He'll have them over for Easter, Thanksgiving. There is a way to make this all work and he's almost there and tomorrow is Monday, a mail day, the letters stacking up, the letters needing time to say the right thing, and the rain run offs his forehead and down his face, slips in to the space between his eyes and his glasses, the lightning banging out over the flatlands' big fields, showing the shadows of silos in the distance. This could be anywhere, he thinks, this could be years ago, this could be a night ten years from now and it would all look the same and his trek could be something he could tell to anyone, ever—he could be unfamiliar with their language and decipher a way with his hands and his eyes and his sounds to tell their story, as it was a story that all knew by heart: the Huns and the Gauls, the Minoans and the Toltec and Great Zimbabweans, because this is what people did both then and now, they found a way to work around life like a bug at a light, taking what warmth they could without getting burned, flying and landing and hoping. It would be a bright day on the Ural and he'd take out a ring, get down on one knee and enter that transaction, that broad history, do it a second time, do it right, do it better. *I'd like to be able to move through the streets*, and he's running now, running to meet her. His socks squish, inside his shoes. Thunder bowls its way down the dark sky's long hall. The world is just clouds and his feet and storm. He turns the street's corner. There's no one there. From back toward the school comes the sound of the train's shrieking whistle.

He's been sitting ten minutes when he sees the headlights of her car, an old black Accord with its rearview missing. He can barely make out her shadowed shape. He can see her pale hands gripping and steering. He looks away, doesn't want to look yet, looks down at the ground, where the grass meets the concrete. She pulls up in front of him, three feet away. For a second he's sure that she'll run him over. She turns the car's lights off but keeps the engine running. It's pouring down rain, the drops hitting the asphalt then jumping. She gets outs. He stands up. His heart is a string, a thin nylon thing that reaches down to his feet and reaches the heavens. His knees don't hurt anymore. She makes him young. She's always done this. He puts his hand on one of the trestle's long beams. He's dizzy with love. He can think of no words. He spent weeks on the words, but he's lost her letter. He arranges his hair into a straight line. Beads of water push over the webs of his fingers and drip down to his neckline, the world just moisture and shadow and sound.

"Hi," she says, and to hear her voice again is to be well for forever.

"Hi," he tells her, and is already moving, already hugging her, her chest against his shirt's FORGOTTONIA decal. He puts his hands on her cheeks. There's something different. He steps back. She's cut off her hair. It's no longer golden. He isn't sure if he's seeing it right. He's living in every moment they've ever had, in every trip that they've been on together. He blinks his eyes. Her hair's a half an inch. She's dyed it brown.

"It's all gone," he says.

"I can't see you," she tells him. "Can we sit in the car?"

He says okay and then grabs her hand, grabs it hard and pumps once and she doesn't pump back and lets go and walks back ahead of him. He walks around to the passenger door. She opens the car and the dome light comes on and he stands there, staring at her through the rain-painted glass. She has on a black t-shirt and oversized jeans. Her shoes are black flats. He hasn't seen them before. He opens the door and sits down and shuts it. She's smiling but meekly, but hardly at all. He leans in to her kiss her and she kisses him back, an arm on his chest, an arm up between them. He tries to open her mouth with his tongue, but she turns away and looks out the window.

"How are you?" she asks. The train sounds again. It's heading west. It's heading toward them.

"I'm good," he tells her, and this is a lie, but he's better now, will only keep getting better. Past the windshield, past the trestle, he stares at the road's end.

"That's good," she says. "Did you hear back yet? From school?"

"I haven't," he says. "Tomorrow, I'm guessing." He's leaning in toward her. She won't look at him. A package of mint gum sits on her dashboard.

"Where'd you get your hair cut?" he asks.

"A friend cut it," she says.

"It looks great," he says, but a flame has gone out. Something inside him has been extinguished. He'll get this back. He thinks of the note. If he had the note, but the storm, but the foxtails.

"I like your hair, too," she says, then looks down at her thighs, at the car seat. The radio's on. Country music is playing. There's a fiddle, a slow slide guitar, a woman crooning about barns and a tree swing and horses. The train sounds again. He's suddenly cold. The car smells of the mint gum and her hair's dampness.

"Presley," he tells her.

"Ian," she says.

His legs have cramped up. Goosebumps dot his arms. The train will be here in a minute, no more. In his head is just the word no, over and over.

"So that's it," he says, but she doesn't answer. Her answer, he thinks, is an archeological one—this culture is dead, here are its ruins.

"Look at me," he says, then says its again, and she says his name but it's raining, there's only the train, the shriek of its whistle taking over the night, the shrill blast making his whole world shake the way that the trestle is shaking, and he hits at the dashboard while his mind breaks, a closed fist, she jumps in her seat, hits it five times, hits it more, the gum falls, she's yelling, his name, and the train's passing over, the metallic clack of its wheels, he's kicking the floorboards, there's no sound or too much of it, snapping against the steel beams, he bangs at the glass, she says get out, she doesn't say this, how could, does she, he is, hitting the windshield, there's knuckles on his blood but that's not right, the order, something went wrong, the world broke, a scene missing, some poor alignment of stars, she's her hands, up and screaming, the train is just sound, and he's tried so hard and this isn't fair and are there seconds where's there's no love in the world at all and he opens the car door and she's crying at him about her dad and the night, except he can't hear it. He gets out of the car. The car drives away. She has made the car drive away. He stands there for ten minutes. He can't seem to think. The rain falls straight down, the wind tired of itself, of its breath, of its pushing.

The headlights coming his way belong to a truck. It parks sideways, over both lanes, twenty yards ahead of him. Its bed is filled with the teenagers he saw before. He's less than alive but more than that, too—a carved idol in a temple she's burned, an old mining camp with all its ore taken. His clothes are so soaked they seem part of his skin. The teenagers hold two-by-fours, baseball bats. Were humans order in a chaotic world? Or was it the reverse? Were humans chaos and once they were all gone, the world could return to how it should be? The rain's pouring down. Someone inside the truck lights a lighter. He starts jogging toward them. He'll swing until he can't. He will keep swinging until he's unconscious. He won't get his job back—he knew this from the start, knew that his time in this town was over. His head hurts. His joints sing with pain. He's fifteen feet away from the sideways-turned vehicle. The teenagers stand there, waiting for him. He runs faster, pumping his arms, pointing his chin out toward them. His fate seems unfair, but he can accept it. He's ten feet away, then only five, the crowd waiting, the bats raised, sneers on their faces. The last thing he sees, before the first fist, is Presley's father. He's sitting in the truck's passenger seat. He rolls down the window and smiles at him. His cigarette smoke trails out into the night. On his hat is the word VIKINGS.

In the spun light of the bright dawn, long bugs cling to the lawn's blades of grass. They are a kind of bug he once knew the name of, but doesn't now. Their bodies are two shades of brown; their bodies are winged and narrow. He leans over his knees on the porch's brick steps. It's stormed through the night but the streets are now dry. It's humid and still. Birds call from trees. In minutes, the sky will no longer be pink. Across the street, past the park, past the bank, a truck's engine whirs, its driver downshifting. The brakes whine then gasp and then the sound's gone, as though the sound never existed.

The bottle of vodka was sitting on the street, on the same block as Shirley Hall and the Provost's large window. He was sure it was water or pee or gasoline, but it wasn't. Its red plastic top was cracked. It was a liter bottle, only the neck gone, the back of it beveled and recessed, for better gripping. He carried it home and stared at it for an hour, feeling the bruises from the boards and the bats sink into his shins and feet, into his forearms and thighs and elbows. Then he'd unscrewed the cap on the bottle.

The sky is impossibly bright. He hasn't felt this good in forever. He thinks that later, when they do the tests, when they cut him open for his post-mortem, it will be too bad that they'll read it all wrong: the loss of his job, his blood alcohol level. They'll set their tack hammers to his levels of earth, look at the cross sections of the trunk of his tree, stare at the rings and make their hypotheses, thinking it a tough year, a fire or a flood, a last tragic epoch in a bountiful era. They'll never know that it's just the reverse—that this moment, now, is more real, is much better.

His neighbor, Smith, walks out of his house. He stands up and says hi and says it too loudly. He half-walks and half-falls down his brick steps. Smith is in his early sixties, older than Presley's dad, who let the others in the truck beat him up and then got out and spat on him. Smith says hello in the early morning light. He has on a plain grey t-shirt and jeans, white running shoes with their laces double-knotted. He can't remember the last time the two spoke. He asks Smith if he can buy a gun from him.

"I'll need some bullets, too," he says.

Smith says I don't think so and then walks away, looking back once before he turns the corner, toward campus. He stands on the lawn, watching his neighbor leave. A minor deterrence. He can fall on a knife. He can let the gas run on the stove in the kitchen. He lights a cigarette as he stands in the grass. For the first time in so long, he feels truly hopeful. What he felt last night was forced, was ersatz. Now, though, a new day and a singular task, a task he can complete, can fully accomplish. He's poured what's left of the vodka into a canteen, an old army thing that had once belonged to his grandfather. It's metal and wrapped in olive green fabric. It has a shoulder strap, which he now slings over his shoulder. He has decided to go for a walk. People do this all the time and he wants to, too. He's feeling great. It's a gorgeous June morning.

He stops at the house where the party was, so long ago. An apprentice of Frank Lloyd Wright built the home; it's cream-colored, three stories, with forest green wainscoting. The driveway is empty of cars. He feels terrifically, impossibly good. He walks on to the house's lawn and begins to rip all of the screens out of the frames of the windows. Some loose themselves easily, peeling away. Others take pulling, take punches. Last night, he put one kid's head hard on the ground, put his knee in his mouth and knocked his teeth out—he found one, after they'd beaten him up, lying there on the road, on the concrete, near the foxtails. He picked the tooth up and began to limp home, then set the incisor down when he'd found the vodka.

He rolls the screens up—there's six of them, total—and sticks them into his frayed shorts' back pocket. One side of his head has a wide ugly gash from where it met with the truck's wheel well, just before he fell and couldn't keep fighting. He touches at it as he walks down the street, then pushes his pink hair over the wound, so no one will see it. He unscrews his canteen, the top attached by a chain. The vodka coats his throat. Birds sing all around him. At the intersection he heads west. Two blocks up, he makes a right, walking down the street that leads to the alley behind her old house. Something in his ankle won't work correctly. He lifts his leg but there's something wrong with the joint, with the bone. Very soon, though, he thinks, this won't really matter.

Gray puddles of rainwater dot the alley's dirt road. Pieces of rubble lie here and there. The light shines in his eyes, the sun straight ahead of him. It occurs to him he's never walked here, before—each time he drove, waiting for her, watching her climb out of the window. She'd drape a leg over, her hands on the sill, then swing her body out, waving at him as she strode toward his Ford, the two of them smiling in anticipation.

The house is for rent; there's no one inside. He takes another sip from his canteen and walks up to the window, touching one finger to the glass. The room past it is bare. He puts his palm to the glass and lifts up. The window jumps an inch in its white wooden frame. Cool air pushes out from under its sill. He swings the canteen behind him, pushes the window up more, climbs inside. They had sex here once, when her roommate was gone. Her mattress was a double that sat on the floor; he can see its vague outline even now, its lingering rectangle. He decides that the canteen is really too full and unscrews its top and turns it upside down, gulping like a runner after a race, like a solider near death, the air filled with mortars, the trench filled with corpses. Both of the bedrooms are on the ground floor, downstairs; he walks toward the front door and peeks in the second, staring at the carpet, at the bare, white walls. He walks up the stairs, to the living room, the bathroom and kitchen. In the last of these places, he turns on the sink and stares at the water that pushes out of the faucet. It occurs to him he'll never see the Pacific again. It will be this place that he knows last of all. It will be this land's set of gods that wrap him in their feathers.

He takes off his canteen, then takes off his glasses, bending down and washing his face. The birdsong is aggressively, wonderfully loud. He turns off the faucet and feels something behind its base. It's a metal barrette, long, thin and grass green. He knows it's hers. It has to be. It's the color of her boots, the boots she wore to class, when he was a professor. He picks it up and puts it in his hair and walks into the bathroom and looks at himself in the mirror. The tape over the side of his glasses is loose; the frames tilt like a funhouse illusion. A single tuft of pink hair sticks past the barrette. His phone rings and he jumps and then says her name, but the call's from a number that he doesn't know. He lets it go. The birds are too loud. The floor of the sky has turned into glass. He can see the gods' feet, now, the shake of their robes. He has enough money left to buy pills that will kill him.

He walks back downstairs but has forgotten the canteen, and as he trudges back up, he feels suddenly tired. He decides to lie down on the kitchen's cool tile. He sets the canteen under his head. It's very hard, but that doesn't matter. He curls his knees up close to his chest. Both of them hurt. Both harbor welts, cuts and bruises. From outside, down the street, a lawnmower starts up; it blends with the sound of the birds, with the sun thrumming in through the kitchen's large window. Hours from now, baseball will be played. Ice cream will melt on the hands of jubilant children. People, on rivers, will steer their small boats. Generations of families will picnic together, the checkered cloth spread out, the dishes and bowls, the breeze warm through the shade of the trees. He stares at the oven then closes his eyes. Something is pressing into his thigh. He reaches into his pocket.

It's the vodka bottle's cap. He puts it over the top of his thumb and sticks his thumb in his mouth and passes out, already dreaming.

It's dark by the time he wakes up. There are stars in the sky. The birds have stopped singing. Everything hurts. He has a headache. He needs to smoke. The room past the kitchen is dark, and he's scared that there's someone in it. His wrists feel hollowed out. Soon, he knows, they'll start shaking. He picks up the empty canteen from the floor. He walks back downstairs, using the wall as a banister. He walks into her room, looks out at the alley. He sees no headlights, sees nothing moving at all. He climbs out and pushes the sill's lip down, behind him. On the walk home, he abandons the screens. They fan out like scrolls in the gutter. The cicadas have started, the air heavy and still. He walks up his porch steps and sticks his hand in the mailbox. There's a single letter, sitting inside. He pulls it out. On its front is a sticky note that says MISDELIVERED. The envelope's from the school—The Office of the President. He opens the door and flips the light on, the walls a bright blue, the gods' lawns turned sideways. He takes off the canteen and rips open the envelope's flap. He stares at the school's watermark, under the ink, beneath words like *restored* and *removed* and *rescinded*. The letter concludes with the phrase *Welcome Back*. He walks outside and stands on his porch, looks out at the park, at the bank that stands past it. His stomach is swimming. His skin feels cold. The bank's ATM glows in the night. The liquor store is open for another five hours. It's a ten-minute walk there. The pharmacy is farther, but it never closes. He can feel the smooth sides of the tamper-proof lid. He can hear the pills clacking inside their container. He's walking. It's night-time. It's summer, late June. One society's doom, he's told class after class, is another's inception.

Rancho Brava

Gloria Inparvo, Vice President
Global Consumer Distribution, S.A.
Research and Development Division
North American Headquarters
317 Industrial Parkway
Milford, CT 06460

Dear Gloria,

Under cover of this letter please find initial, selected results from Global Consumer Distribution's (GCD's) first Focus Group in Zone 5 (Southwest) for Product 1822J: Authentic Garden Fresh Salsa. Focus Group was pre-screened and comprised of qualified members representative of respective geodemographic "groups," per employment of my firm's recently devised classification system, PINON (People In Neighborhoods Or/and Non-neighborhoods), modeled closely on the UK-based demographics system ACORN. (This is not to be confused with the U.S.'s ACORN, a collective of community-based reform organizations that advocated for medium- and low-income families and was destroyed through a range of controversies, nearly all of which were exacted by rich, white men.)

Focus Group was conducted in Banquet Room #3 (The Stardust Room) of the Lubbock, TX, Marriot Hotel on March 4, 2012. Of the fourteen (14) scheduled participants, twelve (12) were present. The remaining two would-be participants, each embroiled in a series of events relating to coincidence, tragedy and pain, indicated in subsequent emails that they would like to be part of another FG in either the near or far future. Light refreshments were made available by the hotel itself, and supplemented by my .8-mile outing to The Hitchin' Post, a combination gas station, grocery store and souvenir shop, and the nearest purveyor of dry, edible goods from the Marriot, where I stayed for two nights in a King Standard.

In an effort of full disclosure, I feel compelled to mention that I am no longer with the firm for which I compiled these data, my intrigue with this part of the country growing so overt following occurrences that transpired during the Focus Group in question that I have chosen to remain here forever. Without any dependents, and following a long and painful divorce from my spouse, one in which my own uxoriousness doomed me to the title of cuckold, I find myself the benefactor of a hefty settlement and owner of a doublewide trailer in Shady Lanes Mobile Court in Levelland, Texas, forty-five minutes from New Mexico's eastern border.

Having been that sort of workaday suburbanite common to much of late 90s/early 00s culture, my desires prosaic, my needs largely met, I've found these recent months and weeks to be akin to standing in a large, circular chamber, its single curving wall covered fully in doors. That is, Gloria, I wake in the morning, make eggs in a pan, put on my water-repellant safari hat with adjustable chinstrap, and venture out into the world, unsure of both where it is that I'm going and when I might return. Have you, Gloria, lived days without predestination, alone in the hot wind and staring out at some distant escarpment, your smart phone in a locked drawer four counties south? What I mean to say is that it's good to feel whole again, and it's you and Global Consumer Distribution, S.A., and the Focus Group in question that I have to thank.

Before proceeding, PINON's classification system, should you not have a copy nearby. Whereas the UK's ACORN system accounts for all of the UK as its single, foundational demographic, PINON subdivides the U.S. regionally, prior to classification; that is, the Southwest Model may look little (or almost exactly) like, say, the Northeast:

PINON 2012 PROFILE DEFINITIONS—ZONE 5: SOUTHWEST*

PINON Types	PINON Groups
A. Thriving	
1.1 Suburbs with Guards and Gates 1.2 Suburbs with Gates 1.3 Suburbs with Implied Gates (e.g., Race, Knowledge of Blue Chips) 2.4 Palatial Livestock Estates 3.5 Bucolic Mountain Top Retreats	1. Madoff Wannabes, Septuagenarians in Golf Carts 2. Gun-toting Mega-Ranchers 3. Sangre de Cristo Trust-Funders
B. Bolstering	
4.6 Those Houses They Show on HGTV That You Could Never Afford 5.7 Houses That Almost Look Like That 6.8 Houses That Will Look Like That Soon	4. God-Fearing, Corner-Office Breeders 5. Ab-Crunching, Work-from-Home, Pagan Techies 6. Nouveau-Riche Construction Moguls
C. Ascending	
7.9 Hip Parts of Town that Were Once Shitty Parts of Town, then Gay Neighborhoods, then Gentrified 8.10 The Student Ghetto 9.11 Innocuous, Curtain-Drawn Split-Levels	7. New Wave Hetero Yuppies with Purse Dogs and Spin Class Memberships 8. Future Versions of 1–7, 9–18. 9. De Facto Cartel Employees, Undercover Department of Justice Workers
D. Sinking	
10.12 Outdated Apartment Complexes with Names Like *Villa Del Sol* and *Spanish Fork Arms* 11.13 Neighborhoods that Used to Look Good but now Might Be the Ghetto	10. Slot Machine Widows, Cactus League Baseball Players 11. The Middle Class (Note: Currently Unclear Whether or Not This Group Still Exists)
E. Toiling	
12.14 Rusting Airstreams 13.15 Crumbling Adobes 14.16 Tarpaper Eyesores	12. Failed Country Singers 13. Deprogrammed Ex-Cult Members 14. Meth-Smoking Oilers with Rap Sheets
F. The Doomed**	
15.17 The Desert 16.18 Basement Efficiencies 17.19 Abandoned School Buses 18.20 Sewers, Caves	15. Drug Mules 16. Pedophiles 17. Section 8 War Veterans 18. Artists, Writers, Intellectuals

*Please note that the Southwest, as a region, remains difficult to *classify* correctly and universally. Arizona and New Mexico, for instance, are nearly always considered the Southwest. However, Texas and Oklahoma are classified by the United States Census Bureau as the South, and not the Southwest nor the West. Furthermore, all the states/regions that at least could be defined as comprising the Southwest—Eastern California, Nevada, Utah,

Colorado, Arizona, and New Mexico—and are not already classified as the "South" (Texas and Oklahoma) are also classified by the Census Bureau as the West, thereby making the Southwest not really a region at all but something closer, perhaps, to *a country of lost borders*, a realm that by title must indeed be a place but also and very much isn't.

**Please note that due to the recent/ongoing recession, portions of many if not all PINON groups normally/otherwise classified as Type A through Type E may now be Type F, The Doomed.

The Zone 5 Focus Group began on time and in orderly fashion. Save for an outdated and innocuous fire exit in the far southeast corner of the room, the chamber was single entranced, with high twin doors of dark wood along its northern wall. These connected to a wide corridor that led in one direction to the spacious if sterile lobby, where at all hours one could find a single member of a rotating cast of clerks in simple black-and-white vestments common to low-level hospitality management employees and, in the other direction, to the two other banquet rooms (The Bluebonnet Room and Rancho Brava), followed by the fitness center and separate, indoor pool. I did not see the interior of either The Bluebonnet Room or Rancho Brava save for pictures on the Lubbock Marriot's well-assembled, no-frills website, one that included virtual tours of all three banquet rooms on the hotel property. The Stardust Room was both the smallest and cheapest of the three offerings, and, as implementation of the Focus Group required no more than a large table, grounded electrical outlet, and space for an old-model television set on a wheeled platform, it (The Stardust Room) was the most logical and cost-effective option.

The room's carpet was a thick, synthetic blend, its primary color cobalt. Strands of reddish brown and bright gray were worked in at regular intervals meant to look random. In providing a type of carpet with this much depth and cushion, I inferred that the room was more often used for social functions than work-related gatherings, as a thinner, more industrial-grade carpet would have sufficed for purposes of the latter but not the former. At the same time, the carpet held so much depth that it would be easy for a new bride to take a postceremony, alcohol-induced tumble—her champagne flute breaking in her palm, a white heel snapping—and as such acts are things no father (or hotel's legal representation) wants, ever, to see, I remained in doubt in regard to whether the room was used more often for business or social occasions.

For Focus Group purposes, the Stardust's Room's only shortcoming—one that did not manifest as such until after the Zone 5 FG had begun, and could not be righted without me stopping the day's event in order to locate a grounds manager, who would in turn have to bring in a second hotel employee to assess and, if possible, repair the problem—was a single, flickering ring of lights on the oversized wooden fixture closest to the room's main door. Much like the tufts of ochre and gray in the carpet, these fixtures were spaced around the room in a pattern meant to seem random but that was in truth governed by precise measurements chosen in order to arrive at a specific desired effect. Totaling nine, each fixture was, by design, a wagon wheel, though it was impossible for me to tell whether or not these wagon wheels were, at one point, just that—spoked wooden circles that sat astride some Concord's thoroughbraces, its buggy lurching like a wounded gunfighter through the thick desert dust, toward a Sierra boomtown—and had been repurposed, or, alternately, if these wheels were new and only designed to look as though they were antique.

In either case, and as I have mentioned, the lights (twelve in total) on the fixture that hung nearly over the threshold of the entrance to The Stardust Room were faulty, sizzling on and off in a manner akin to poorly functioning neon tubes comprising a sign for any mode of seedy drinking establishment. Spread out over the oval-shaped table—the kind found most often in corporate boardrooms, the wood particleboard under a thick synthetic gloss—were my firm's preconceived Focus Group packets, which would accompany the interview conducted by myself. Fifteen chairs ringed the table: fourteen for the total number of planned participants and one for myself, though I would not sit down over the course of the day. Off-brand bottled water stood next to each packet. As the participants arrived I moved from my spot next to the television set on one side of the table to its other end, introducing myself and extending a hand, palm up, toward the folding table of refreshments on the western side of the room. Included there were two cheese and fruit platters (hotel-bought), an array of soft drinks and sparkling fruit juices, and more bottled water of the same (non) brand, in addition to the items I purchased at the aforementioned Hitchin' Post. These included foil-wrapped plastic sleeves of cream-filled chocolate cookies, two packages of name-brand butter crackers, one bag of bite-sized chocolate candies (assorted), and fifteen strips of what the cylindrical plastic container next to the Hitchin' Post's cash register called "boar jerky," the nomenclature declaring that the rough-hewn strips of preserved meat were indeed dried slabs of wild pig. (Upon closer inspection of the container itself, this turned out, as imagined, to be false, the jerky not that of a dead wild pig, but rather the flesh of cattle, the inference being, Gloria, that lies of a certain shape and size are perfectly acceptable in the realm of food marketing.)

With small talk accomplished and seats at the table taken, the Focus Group pushed on to the task at hand, namely identifying what they found compelling about the array of salsa products currently on the market, in addition to their broader, respective convictions on salsa itself. At the outset, and per GCD's corporate guidelines, I read the Informed Consent Form in its entirety:

Welcome Statement

Welcome! You are here today in order to participate in a discussion about salsa. On behalf of Global Consumer Distribution, S.A., I would like to thank you for your participation. Everything you say here will be confidential. We will be recording this discussion. If you can take a moment, now, to sign the waiver sheet indicating that executives at Global Consumer Distribution have the right to read this material and make use of it in appropriate, business-driven ways, it would be appreciated. We'll pause for thirty seconds while you read through the waiver form then sign and print your name, initialing where it is mandated you do so. Your participation in this focus group is entirely voluntary. Your opinions are important to us. You will not be paid.

(Thirty second pause.)*

*(This pause, Gloria, was actually much longer than thirty seconds. While I won't include a copy of the waiver form here, you and I both know that the average individual, and even a high-functioning one, would have trouble reading with clarity and precision a three-page form in 10-pt type

with anything approaching lucidity in the time allotted, especially when said form is laden with byzantine legalese. Please do not understand my actions as either roguish or attempting to establish ideology dichotomic [i.e., humanism vs. corporate fascism] in nature. Rather, it simply seemed to me that in thirty seconds no one was going to get this done.)

After this introductory message and the signing and collecting of consent forms, and per GCD's FG guidelines, I had each member of the FG state his or her name and offer whatever brief details about him- or herself they would like to, in addition to what their favorite type of salsa was. Personal details, in some cases, lasted as much as three minutes, and there was a direct correlation between level of faith in a Christian God and lack of brevity in speaking of one's self. Favorite salsas ranged from restaurant to homemade to store bought. At this point, I had FG Participants flip past the cover page of their FG packets and focus on the first question therein:

Question One—On a scale of 1 to 10, how fully do you associate salsa as being that food most emblematic of the Southwestern United States, with 1 being not at all and 10 being the most representative of all foods in existence?

Responses—As anticipated by GCD, responses here were high, with the average being 8.12. The highest response was a 10, and the lowest was a 3, a single member of the Focus Group arguing that salsa actually had nothing to do with the United States, was Latin in origin, and therefore could not be emblematic of any U.S. region. This led to the first of many tête-à-têtes over the course of the day, with the FG Participant who argued this point initially meeting harsh criticism from a second FG Participant, who contended that, by saying salsa was not at all American, Latinos and Latin Americans had nothing to do with American culture. The original FG Participant defended the original point posed, adding that embedded in the retort was an implication of racism, something that the first FG Participant would not stand for. At this point, most of the other Focus Group Participants, unsure of what to think about the points raised and, in a fashion typical to the current era of American social critique and debate, went mute and grew very uncomfortable; there was much shifting in chairs and rearranging of small mounds of snacks on the paper plates in front of members of the group in their attempts to reaffirm that (a) the group has the right to be left out of participating in non–salsa-related discourse and (b) their provisions (i.e., the snack mounds) would not be taken from them. For your purposes, though, Gloria, the point is moot, as per GCD's FG guidelines, lowest and highest scores were omitted.

Question Two—When thinking about authenticity, and how the term relates to spicy, sometimes tomato-based, sauces, what comes to mind?

Responses—As anticipated by GCD, "fresh tomatoes" was the most common response. In other words, the language in the posed question did indeed do its job in functioning as mental suggestion to almost the entire FG. Exceptions to this rule fell well in the realm of logic, and included "salsa that was prepared within hours of eating it" and "salsa without preservatives" and the surprisingly informed "salsa with tomatoes that have not been heat processed," although in many ways all of these responses were an alternate way of saying the most common one. Data collected for Question Two keep in line with data collected from other Question Twos posed in other regions, where the phrase "sometimes tomato based" was substituted for "sometimes chili based." That is, Gloria, whatever mode of narrative is established by the perceived authority is the one maintained by the demographic in the perceived subordinate position. Nearly always, we eat what we are fed. It seems, too, that there may not be a need on the part of Global Consumer Distribution, S.A., to include the phrase "Garden Fresh" on the labeling of Product 1822J (i.e., the salsa), as for the majority of FG Participants in Zone 5, "Authentic" seemed to imply "Garden Fresh," and I am imagining that leaving this phrase out of 1822J's labeling has the potential to be cost saving. To say this another way, it seems that for most in Zone 5, for something to be genuine, it must also, interestingly, be recent.

Question Three—In keeping on the topic of authenticity, how important is it to you as consumers that your salsa be "authentic," with a 1 response indicating not important at all and a 10 response indicating that you in all likelihood would not purchase and/or eat the salsa in question, were it not authentic?

Responses—Data were inconclusive, with the mean response being a 5.71.

Preemptively, FG Participants began to discuss *cost*, the theme of the back-and-forth being that one must indeed "shell out more to get the real deal," while the group's counterpoint was perhaps best summed up by the phrase "but some of that store-bought shit tastes real enough." (At this point I was asked by one of the FG Participants with a strong inclination toward the Christian God [and the most long-winded talker of all FG Participants, at the FG's outset] to maintain discussion guidelines that would disallow for the use of profanity amongst all FG Participants. The utterer of the profane word in turn issued an apology, and this seemed to set things right.) So, while opinion varied greatly on importance of authenticity (which, one could conclude from Question Two, also signifies newness), there did seem to be agreement on the idea that the more genuine and original the product was, the greater the expense incurred by the consumer. One could apply such thinking to a great many number of products offered on the free market—say, for instance, books. One is left to wonder, Gloria, in regard to books, what type of market shift might arise were it epic novels of contemporary literary fiction that were to be placed on the shelves of big box stores and priced competitively, as opposed to bawdy romances and spy thrillers. How would the world change?

Most importantly, and as response discussion of Question Three dwindled, much like the dulling embers of a cowboy's dying fire as the sun rises over the desert's red dirt, the first of a series of events (the ones I mentioned prior) would introduce itself to the Zone 5 Focus Group and forever and irrevocably alter both the day's events and my life. What happened precisely, Gloria, was that Davey Crockett walked into the Zone 5 Focus Group.

As one FG participant concluded extolling the virtues of homemade, hand-crafted salsa, and a second FG Participant countered that notion, saying that even if the food was indeed homemade and handcrafted, the ingredients used—specifically, the tomatoes, the cilantro, the chilies, the corn, etc.—were in all likelihood GMFs, and therefore grown in labs and/or corporate fields where all manner of manmade chemical was added to the water sprayed onto the already toxin-steeped soil from which the array of vegetables grew, and therefore the "homemade" and "handcrafted" salsa could in no way be seen as authentic because the ingredients comprising the salsa would not be genuine ingredients but rather function as ersatz, and necessarily not taste anything like how salsa tasted, say, during the 19th Century, pre-GMFs—as this conversation was winding itself down, Gloria, the lights on the wagon wheel fixture above the door began to buzz and strobe and a younger man of Anglo descent, wearing a suede, fringed blouse, ecru leggings, and a coonskin cap with a tail trailing down one side of it, much in the manner of a tassel of a hat one wears on the day they receive a degree from an institution of learning, entered The Stardust Room.

The room's twin doors had levered handles on both their exterior and interior sides, but as is often the case with doors in environments such as banquet rooms (or, say, divorce lawyers' offices) only one of the two doors actually opened, the non-opening door being both top- and bottom-latched in a manner where the levered handle itself would turn, making one believe that they had made progress in their attempt at entering the room, only to find that the door itself would not budge. This unintentional trick is one that I have always found consternating, Gloria, not only because it mandates that for a few seconds the individual entrant is made to feel embarrassed by the fact that, as a fully grown adult, he/she has yet to master how to enter a room, but also that the exact movement that the combination of the turning handle and non-moving door puts into play is one that has the potential to be truly injurious. Here's what I mean: not knowing that the door won't move once the levered handle is turned, the average would-be room-enterer continues to lean toward the door in question, while at the same time continuing to press down on the levered handle. Were the door indeed to open, or the handle itself to remain in a non-moving and locked position, the pressure on the wrist and elbow joints of the would-be opener would be alleviated by either/both the swinging motion of the door or the stasis of the handle. However, since there is no way for the door to move, the turner of the handle is forced to continue with the motion of blind depression, forcing his/her body ever closer to the threshold until the handle reaches the limit of its rotation, at which point, often, the individual trying to enter the room has wound up in an extremely awkward and potentially painful position.

I mention this action in the detail that I do as Davey Crockett himself was involved in it, prior to his appearance under the flickering ring of lights very near The Stardust Room's entrance. The locked door's handle turned, then turned again, and then, after a beat of one-two, Davey Crockett tried and succeeded at opening the door that would open. Crockett took three steps into the banquet room and stopped, looking around, a grin on his face, this facial expression then changing, in the proceeding seconds, to a look of confusion and minor bereavement—Crockett's eyes pulled down, and he swung his head side to side, the tail of the coonskin cap swinging to-and-fro as though the animal for which the hat had been named had reanimated, and found the moment to be one of pronounced excitement. Suffice to say, Gloria, that all talk of authenticity and newness in relation to salsa ceased as our group stared at the long-dead American frontiersman.

As Focus Group Leader and temporary, ad hoc GCD representative, responsibility fell upon myself to make sure that the day's overarching event would not be interrupted to the extent that the FG Participants misremembered why it was that they were there in the first place. That is, after Crockett failed to turn around and leave the room on his own, so that we as a group might return to our discussion of authentic, southwestern salsas, I offered up a very polite and tactful May I Help You. Crockett, staring at the partially consumed spread of food along the western wall, then looked at me, asking Is This Rancho Brava? At this juncture, many of the FG Participants turned their heads from Crockett toward me, seemingly unsure of the correct answer. I informed Crockett (and, by extension, those members of the group) that it was not, at which juncture Crockett raised a hand in apology, spun around on one foot, and exited The Stardust Room forever.

While at the surface seemingly intrusive, the arrival and departure of Davey Crockett from the Focus Group did, in the short term, wind up being advantageous, as the pioneer's cameo translated ultimately to a moment of bonding amongst the FG Participants. Having collectively witnessed an event that none of the group imagined having any possibility of witnessing, a friendly camaraderie washed over the recent strangers, so much so that a light spell of chuckling made its way around our oval-shaped table. Soon after this, the light fixture's wiring righted itself, and the bulbs above the door stopped their flickering. I did my best to let the moment's minor joy play itself out, then directed GCD's FG Participants back to 1822J's discussion packet.

Question Four—Turning our focus, now, to the packaging of salsa products, and specifically the sort of packaging that you, as consumers, perceive as being visually representative of "an authentic, garden fresh, southwestern salsa," I'd like to direct your attention to the television next to me, asking that you pay close attention to the three different salsa labels shown on the video. As you look at these three different labels, I would like you to keep mental notes of those images or portions of images that reveal themselves to you as authentic and/or garden fresh and/or southwestern. If you would like to take notes on scratch paper, please raise your hand now.

Ten of the twelve FG Participants raised their hands, and I made my way around our table with two boxes, one containing pieces of blank, looseleaf paper (cut in half by a paper cutter that sat, somewhat surprisingly, on a low table directly behind the Marriot's front desk counter) and another, smaller box containing well-sharpened, half-length, eraserless pencils. With these implements administered, I returned to my spot next to my unused seat and, per GCD's guidelines, verbally indicated that I would now turn on the television (though in truth the act itself would seem just as effectively to indicate such). With this announcement, a certain bristling of anticipation—one truly palpable—arose from the majority of the FG Participants, and there was much repositioning of bodies in chairs and rustling of papers and tapping of pencils against the synthetically glossed table. That is, Gloria, I had the sense that the FG Participants believed themselves, as the saying goes, in for a real treat, even though the extent of what we would be doing involved no more than staring at three, twenty-second videos of salsa jars. As I type this letter, I have not truly sat down and taken in television programming for over three months, so much so that when I happen upon one, in a restaurant/bar or department store or other establishment, I find myself, compared to my former, TV-watching days, both far more repulsed and intrigued by the technology and its programs. It seems to me that not having such a machine in one's home makes said machine seem out of place truly everywhere, and consistently I find myself perplexed by and yet nonetheless drawn to the set in the aforementioned public places, though this psychological reaction may be no different, in truth, from a moth being drawn to a blinking and sound-producing bug light of the kind whose singular purpose is ultimately to kill those attracted to it.

The Stardust Room's grounded outlet was in perfect working order, and, prior to the arrival of the FG Participants, I had cued the tape to the appropriate, beginning moment of the video. The first salsa jar on display was Label Model 3B: Cowboy on Horse at Sunset. To remind, this is the same front image as Label Models 3A, 3C, and 3D, with time of day the single variable. (3A being Cowboy on Horse [CoH] at Sunrise, 3C being CoH in Nighttime and 3D being CoH at High Noon.) All FG Participants were attentive and respectful of the attentiveness of others in the opening moments of the video, but then, Gloria, at 3B's halfway point, an AP (Anticipated Problem) arose. The AP in question dealt with the woman's hand descending into the shot of the salsa jar, and turning said jar so that FG Participants could view the rear half of the label.

As the FG Participants took notes (some copious) on their pieces of scratch paper with their uncomfortable, miniature pencils, looking from the screen to their paper and back to the screen again, the AP (the woman's hand) descended, interrupting the pristine white background in front of which the jar of salsa sat. Its skin pale, its nails unpainted, its fingers lithe if not truly graceful, the hand moved at a consistent rate, from the northwest corner of the shot to only, barely, the top edges of 1822J, never once pausing, even after contact with the lid had been made, even after the motion of turning the jar had begun, even after the hand had completed turning the jar and raised itself away from the product, lifting out of the shot at that same constant motion. It was a rate of sincere professionalism, one not fast but also not slow, a rate that understood the task at hand and also its place in the moment's larger context.

I hadn't seen my wife's hand in so long, Gloria (roughly six months), and to witness it, then, as the FG Participants cooed at its arrival, was like my own thoughts had been transferred into the mouths of the others in the room, their small sounds of wonder not unlike the murmurs of awe that escaped past my former betrothed's lips while we stood gazing up at the frescoed ceiling of the Sistine Chapel, on our honeymoon. That the AP (my wife's hand) descended into the video of the salsa at roughly the same angle that Adam holds his hand in the creation scene on that famous, frescoed ceiling in order to attain his Breath of Life from Michelangelo's God was a truth that had not arrived to me prior to that moment in The Stardust Room, and while the FG Participants scribbled and buzzed, I was forced to consider, again, my past failures at love, shortcomings earned by my former self via placing belief in the dual (and sometimes overlapping) concepts of faith and union, even when such placing of belief overrode logic. That is, Gloria, I really did convince myself that my wife was fixing a male friend's boots, when I found said footwear in her closet one summer evening, and I really did convince myself that my wife, feeling suffocated by our shared domesticity, needed "more nights out with the girls," and I really did convince myself, Gloria, I really, really did, that upon finding condoms in the drawer of my wife's nightstand one Sunday afternoon, while cleaning the upstairs of our mortgaged American Colonial, there was a well-intentioned reason for the sheath of contraceptives, so much so that the thing to do, as opposed to asking my wife about them, was simply to repair the chain of condoms to the trash and never once, ever, mention their presence.

Gloria, are you familiar with Michelangelo's Creation of Adam? On that part of the Chapel's ceiling, behind the image of God, is an open, swirling cloak, painted maroon. It was noted by a doctor in the American Midwest, some years ago, that this cloak, billowing and packed full of human figures and other shapes, is an anatomically correct picture of the human brain, with the figures and shapes serving as visual representations of all manner of lobes and glands and sulci, and the cloak itself providing the outline of the nervous system's most vital organ. One could infer from such a notation that behind even a premiere personification of faith and belief, there must be logic, Gloria—that to wish blindly is no more than folly or curse, and to pray without thinking is the work—in the Christian tradition—of the Devil.

The Focus Group carried on without such thoughts in their heads, invested as they were in the colors of Label 3B, and the attractiveness of the shadow of a cowboy and horse, alone in the desert at sunset. After this shot ended, the next one began, my wife's hand descending to the lid of Label 5B (Coyote Baying at Moon) and Label 6A (Prospector Crouched Next to River), the FG Participants making their notes, a single member of the group speculating aloud, I Wonder How Much They Pay the Hand to Do That. This was met by a chuckle then a shushing, I, all the while, dying inside, and then, Gloria, for the second time that day, the lights on the wagon wheel nearest the door began to flicker.

The mariachi octet that entered the room, accidentally serenading the FG Participants and myself, was an outfit named Mariachi Errante. I've seen them twice since the day at the hotel, running into the band, completely coincidentally, at a street festival in Santa Fe and later a trilevel parking garage in El Paso. At the second of these locations, Errante's van had broken down, though the problem was actually nothing more than a corroded distributor cap, and one that I could easily remedy. As I worked, the vihuela player and I talked a bit, conversing in that manner frequent to male strangers with little in common between them. For instance, Luis (the vihuela player) asked me if I was married, and I told him that I once had been. He asked me if I had children, and I told him that I didn't. With these questions asked (and there is a certain bravery in the asking, Gloria, a certain putting out there of one's self in a way that appears casual but is actually suffused with risk, much in the way that a professional poker player slides his/her full stack forward, across the table's green felt, lips set, hands calm, insides screaming from the madness of the gambit while knowing, also, that it's the way that the game must be played) and answered, I counter-volleyed, asking the identical questions of Luis, who had very different answers from my own, combining the two responses into a single, longer one that spanned the rest of my switching out of the corroded distributor cap and involved a soccer match, a long-standing family feud, a child's finger lost to a scorpion sting, the Department of Homeland Security, a stolen trumpet, the smell of dried chilies ground in a mortar and pestle, wet sand under bare feet that the warm surf washed across in a calming, rhythmic way, coyotes of the human kind, coyotes of the non-human kind, a Zeta-owned cantina in Douglas, AZ, an outmoded six-shooter that went off in someone's hand, and a choice made outside a supermarket in St. George that would haunt Luis and the rest of the mariachi band forever. Wiping at my oil-striped hands with a rag that one of Errante's violin players produced, I told Luis that that was quite a story, a statement that made Luis shrug and then say, it is only how life can be, Roberto.

I of course knew none of this that day at the Marriott, the octet, one by one, entering through the single opening door of The Stardust Room (an act that with eight people really took some time, though the band began playing and singing as soon as their first member crossed the room's threshold), and instead could only listen, as the other FG Participants did, to the melodramatic and bittersweet sentiments of the song sung by the group, a number of which they played the entirety, and which elicited genuine applause from the FG Participants, some of whom then looked to me, assuming that I had planned the intermission. This incorrect hypothesis was understood in full once the octet had repaired their instruments to a non-playing position, Luis (the unspoken but clear leader of the band) asking, Is This Rancho Brava? I informed Mariachi Errante that it was not, and, in uniform motion, the eight men then bowed, walking out of The Stardust Room and leaving myself and the FG Participants in a silence so complete it was as though we had just sat through an earthquake. Luis, the last band member to exit the room, turned around to face us as he closed the door, nodding his head in departure and apology. Three seconds later, the lights on the wagon wheel fixture stopped their flickering.

The Zone 5 Focus Group was, much to their credit, Gloria, able to regain focus after this unexpected interlude, and return once more to the task at hand, mentally filing away both the mariachi band and Davey Crockett. Cowboy on Horse at Sunset scored the highest of the three labels shown, with Prospector Crouched Next to River edging out Coyote Baying at Moon, the inference being, perhaps, that people are more attracted to images of people than images of animals but most appreciate images that contain both people and animals functioning in tandem. Alternately, Gloria, the case could be made that the FG's choosing of the Cowboy on Horse at Sunset label had actually nothing to do with the cowboy or the horse at all, and only the sunset, that time of day when people are often the most contemplative, and, being thrust into an environment of forced contemplation (i.e., the Focus Group), the Participants' immediate confines greatly affected their decision-making process. However, if we look at current trends in other industries—say, for instance, the publishing industry—we see a clear and strong movement toward the placing of a person or people on book covers, especially in cases of bawdy romances and young adult crossover fiction, those industry areas with some of the largest market share. Indeed, even in industry areas with very low sales, so much so that these areas are largely *financially worthless* (for instance, literary fiction), one can see a trend toward the placing of people on the cover of titles, perhaps in the attempt to have the design of the book lure people into buying them through something akin to *empathy*, the unstated belief being, on the part of the industry's respective marketing departments, that a more figurative and perhaps "artistic" design—say, for instance, an empty banquet room, with only a TV, some chairs, and a table beneath wagon wheel light fixtures—would be too sterile and too dissociative to hold the hypothetical consumer's attention long enough for said consumer to pick the book up off the big box store's shelf, look at the cover, flip the book over to its back cover (where another human-based image would be), and decide, all in a span of five seconds, to place the book in his/her oversized cart, along with food products, toiletry items, and those products that serve no purpose at all past entertainment and whimsy. As stated prior, Gloria, we eat what we're fed, and those items that we choose to eat are, for the most part, marketed directly toward *short-term gratification,* despite being in direct, ironic opposition to the indefatigable truth that if all one consumes is snack cakes, frozen pizza, and sugary, carbonated beverages, the marketer will be unable, long-term, to market toward that consumer, because, Gloria, that consumer will be *dead*, due in large part to the prior successes of the marketer. But the notion of the sustainable consumer, as we both know, is folly, as that consumer necessarily ages and dies, in the meantime copulating and reproducing and ultimately spawning offspring that can replace them. Therefore, the idea, on the marketer's end, of long-term betterment of the consumer can only be a fool's game. How do you make broccoli sexy, Gloria? You do not. There is no way on Earth to make broccoli sexy.

Gloria, here is the section of the text where I would list Question Five, that question dealing with the perceived, correct viscosity of authentic, garden fresh salsa—should it be thick? Should it be runny? How much xantham gum and sodium alginate should be injected into the vat of vegetable slurry and stirred by factory machines, in order to provide an authentic, garden fresh salsa experience, one that will be able to be enjoyed repeatedly, even after the consumer has picked up and set down the salsa a half dozen times from a white, barred shelf of their refrigerator? An important concern, to be sure, but one, too, that was overridden by the continuing, escalating series of events that had already been set in motion prior to the FG's consideration of how thick or not thick a salsa's "body" should be in order to be authentic. (Gloria, as I write this a Gila monster has perched itself on a rock, just past my doublewide's west-facing window. It's striped pink and brown and nearly two feet in length and its body looks like some bit of bright, banded reef removed from the sea and set next to my trailer. I have seen, too, a horned frog shoot blood from its eyes. I have seen also a dust storm black out the noon sun, turning the world to nothing but grit, sound, and darkness.)

As the Group centered its attention to the correct thickness of 1822J, and truly no more than seconds after I had asked the question out loud to the Zone 5 FG Participants, the lights on the wagon wheel flickered again, and the door of The Stardust Room opened. Initially, all that appeared in the threshold was a brown and white cowboy boot with a spur attached to it. The spur—replete with rowels, chap guards, and metal buttons for straps—tinkled lightly against The Stardust's Room synthetic carpet, the dual noises of the door opening and the bright ting of the boot's accessory enough to steal away the attention of the FG Participants. The owner of the boot/spur, who followed his footwear into the room some theatrically long seconds after, was a narrow-hipped, Caucasian man in a tan, ten-gallon hat and tan vest worn over a white, long-sleeved shirt with a banded, buttoned collar. His tan jeans were tight on his thin legs, and attached to the lapel of his vest was a large, gold badge comprised of a star with a circle around it. The man was in his late fifties, perhaps, with small, dark eyes under wide, salt-and-pepper eyebrows. His most striking feature, though, Gloria, by far, was his enormous mustache.

From the man's flume to either side of his mouth, all the way down to his jaw line, the mustache, a bright silver, was two inches thick, the hairs long enough that one couldn't see the man's lips—either upper or lower—in the slightest. At exactly those twin points where the mustache passed the edges of the man's jaw, the silver hairs had been waxed and forced to curl both up and back, toward the stranger's cheekbones. The man's chin was short, with a pronounced cleft, its anatomical meekness lessened all the more by the profound ornament of facial hair that framed it, so much so that the would-be sheriff's face seemed merely a host for the organism that was the mustache. Indeed, and as the man strode (truly strode, Gloria, leading with his hips, the upper half of his torso [purposefully or not] tilted back behind them) farther into the room, the parts comprising his costume (i.e., the sheriff's badge, the ten-gallon hat, the tinging, metal spurs, the impossible mustache) superseded all other aspects of his humanity, so much so that the costume he wore became who he was *in toto*. That is, Gloria, it was truly impossible to imagine the marshal in a vast majority of contemporary settings, say for instance, sliding down a slide at a water park, or waiting in line to renew his car's registration at the Department of Motor Vehicles. (Of course, now that I have written what I just have, Gloria, it *does* become possible to imagine the sheriff in both of the aforementioned settings; the *actual* difficulty involved with such an imagining is that in either scenario, the sheriff—at least for me—is still wearing portions of his costume. While it makes no legitimate sense for the lawman to remain in his ten-gallon hat and cowboy boots and spurs as he schusses down a plastic, reinforced slide into a pool filled with screaming children, in my mind, Gloria, he is—he still has the hat on, and the boots, and the spurs, his bright, pale knees and lower thighs in stark contrast to the leather of the footwear and his shorts-length, drawstring swimsuit. [Which, in my imagining, Gloria, is the very same maroon as the swirling cloak encompassing the image of God on the ceiling of the Sistine Chapel.])

As the sheriff swaggered closer, across the padded cobalt floor, coming farther into the room than either Davey Crockett or the mariachi octet had prior, I began to perceive the past hour's major events—the Focus Group about salsa, the costumed strangers, my wife's hand—as not unrelated points in space, but rather a trio of vertices, the rays adjoining these points uniform in length and comprising, Gloria, an equilateral triangle. Staring blatantly at the man's massive facial hair (the mustache was like a bug, like a live, furry thing that at any moment might choose an alternate place to rest its wide frame and rip free from the man's face, fall to the floor, and scuttle toward one of the banquet room's corners), I found that I was drawing into myself, and that the room's minor sounds (the tinging of the spurs, the barely perceptible whine of the paused DVD, the Focus Group's murmurs) had dampened. It was at this time that I began to sketch, at some desk in my mind, something akin to a primitive seesaw. While both ends of the saw's lever were empty of any sort of physical being, the long, brown board was conceptually inhabited, respectively, by authenticity and counterfeit. The fulcrum—a golden triangle—sat accordingly, underneath, and at each of its corners now appeared a different image: pico de gallo in a crude, three-legged bowl, a gunslinger in chaps holding twin six-shooters, and my wife, standing in our old living room, covering the mouthpiece of her cell phone as she spoke into it. The sheriff took two more steps forward and then stopped, setting his legs even farther apart and then placing his hands on his hips as he took in the stares of the Focus Group Participants, who by this point, Gloria, I was aware of in only a minor, ethereal way, their heads—turned away from me and toward the man—seeming to float in the air, disembodied.

As I continued to stare at the mustache's wiry, fibrous hairs (I think I was smiling a tactful, professional smile, Gloria, but I can't be sure of it), I grew cognizant of the illegitimacy of the device that I had, in my mind, just constructed. Here's what I mean: the image attached to each of the triangle's points—the pico de gallo, the chaps-wearing outlaw, and the person to which I used to be married—could not possibly function as anything fulcrum-esque, as at least some approximation of all three of the images my mind had conjured up were currently being weighed for their validity: a salsa's correct thickness being scrutinized by the members of the FG, the genuineness of my former union by me, and the veracity of the strangers who entered The Stardust Room being measured, I believe, by all present. If these images, then, were not balanced at all, but rather variables in need of accurate weighing, it drew into question (at least for me) what face, shape, or thing might universally serve as a true midway point for the beam of the seesaw. (And image-based vertices felt vital, Gloria, as without them the fulcrum was a fulcrum by title, and no more, much in the same way that a corrupt or deceitful buyer of gold might rig his or her own scale in order to show a correct balance. [I saw a similar thing occur on an excursion to Taos, where an elderly woman clad in a batik dress of earth tones, while buying a sizable amount of pork chops at a butcher's counter inside a supermarket, calmly slid her tri-folded grocery list under the polished, silver top of the butcher's electronic scale while the butcher himself was not looking, the woman effectively rigging the machine in order to make the pork chops' combined weight, when measured, seem lighter.])

Meanwhile, as the seesaw I'd constructed clattered apart, the unannounced sheriff took his right hand from his hip and waved in a wide and deliberate manner to his new, sudden audience. The action's velocity, already theatrically slow, was to my perception further reduced by my own internal postulations, and, as the sheriff began speaking, his words arrived at such a diminished rate that they barely seemed to be words at all, and something closer, perhaps, to a type of alien soundscape, each phoneme drawn out to the length of multiple syllables, my mind in some way aware of the fact that what the sheriff was saying was the same question that had been asked twice prior that day (specifically, Is This Rancho Brava?), but the query arriving as something closer to:

IIIIIIIIIIIIIIIIIIIIIIIIIIIIIIIIIIIIIIIIIIIIIIIIIIIIIIIIIIIIIIII-
IIIIIIIIIIIIIIIIIIIIIIIIIIIIIIIIIIIIIIIIIIIIIIIIISSSSSSSSSSSSSSSSSSSS-
THIIIIIIIIIIIIIIIIIIIIIIIIIIIIIIIIIIIIIIIIIIIIISSSSSSSSSSSSSSSSSSSS-
RRRRRRRRRRRRAAAAAAAAAAAAAAAAAAAAAAAAAANNNN-
CHOOOOOOOOOOOOOOOOOOOOOOOOOOOOOOOOOO-
BRRRRRRRRRRRRRRAAAAAAAAAAAAAAAAAAAAAAAA-
VVVAAAAAAAAAAAAAAAAAAAAA?

As I gave my response (It Is Not), the acts of the room returned to a normal pace, the sheriff tipping his hat, whirling around, and striding back out the same door through which he had entered. However, Gloria, with the sheriff's departure and the wagon wheel's lights again on, and as I attempted to return to functioning in the manner my title dictated, I noticed that the attitude of the Focus Group Participants had changed in a way that, for the purposes of Global Consumer Distribution, S.A., was not beneficial. That is, Gloria, while the individuals comprising the Zone 5 FG had been able to see both Crockett and the mariachi band as minor if amusing distractions, the arrival and departure of the sheriff brought about a movement away from the scientific inquiry of my salsa-based questions, the socio-intellectual overtones of the FG replaced with discussion (and something approaching love for) the notion that the sheriff had created his mustache from nothing, eschewing the general facial-hair "rules" of our time that dictated what a mustache should or should not consist of, his folksy, enormous, barbed crescent of hairs elevated to something more important and profound than our shared rationalization of what elements comprise an unassailably authentic snack product.

Furthermore, Gloria, this shared enthusiastic response to the sheriff's grooming choices (perhaps best and most appropriately summarized by one member of the FG proclaiming Dude's Mustache Was The Bomb) also spelled a change wherein the Zone 5 FG chose to place its loyalties. If I, as contractually obligated leader of our small group, was to this point afforded the authority inherent in such a title, the Focus Group's feelings toward the constraints that my quasi-aristocratic role ostensibly placed upon them grew increasingly aggressive as I tried to maintain/exert/reestablish order. Okay, let's focus, I would say to the group, but the group, Gloria, would only keep talking, until even that FG Participant with the strongest proclivity toward the Christian God snapped her head toward me, her stare meaning revolt, and said, We're Speakin' Here, And You Ain't Even Texan.

This painting of myself as something approaching hegemon or paramount king induced flashpoint in the other members of the Focus Group, and, if previously aware of yet indifferent toward the contrast in our respective regions of origin, the FG Participants now seized upon it, asking me a bevy of questions that had nothing to do with my dual, overlapping roles as Global Consumer Distribution, S.A. Representative and Zone 5 Focus Group Leader. For instance, upon learning that I'd grown up in a Virginia suburb of Washington, DC, one Focus Group member proffered aloud that I worked not for Global Consumer Distribution at all, and instead for the Central Intelligence Agency, the FG itself having nothing to do with the perceived correctness of snack foods and much more to do with an unspecified mode of government spying. Further diminishing my credibility were the facts that: (1) I had never been to a barrel race, (2) I did not know that Angelo light slaughters were trading ten dollars lower, (3) recent advents in baler technology were lost upon me, (4) I couldn't accurately define *asado*, and (5) when asked of my favorite country song, I could not offer the title of *any* such warbling ballad, leading one FG Participant actually to snort, then conclude that The Feds Trained [Me] Crummy.

With my interrogation complete (there were questions, Gloria, about my hunting rifle of choice, about my theological and sexual orientations, about whether my parents were "Flag-Burning Hippy Pigs," about whether I rooted for or against the Dallas Cowboys when they played on Thanksgiving), the Focus Group, freed from my apparently tyrannical rule and drunk on some primordialist cocktail comprised of equal parts xenophobia and newfound liberation, began to offer up a list of demands, most of which dealt with, in some way, shape, or form, going outside, into Nature. I informed the FG that their requests could not be met, as we still had forty-five more questions about salsa to go (forty-six if one were to include the only partially completed question about Salsa Thickness.)

This response elicited a long round of moans from the FG Participants, their collective auditory chagrin something akin to the sound one might hear rising out of a pulverized battlefield trench, mustard gas roiling about in the air, the treads of a tank whirring just past the dirt lip of the Focus Group's battered excavation. Every society, however, is forced to progress, even if they destroy portions of themselves to do it, even if questions of worth and importance (e.g., if the artist's feelings are his law, was the sheriff's art [i.e., his mustache] an accurate extension of his own feelings?) go unanswered. That is, Gloria, we persisted. We pressed on. We took those preconceived, established notions of salsa and blew them apart, reconfiguring where salsa should sit on a shelf and what aisle, in a store, the salsa should be in. We rewrote and reprised. We made salsa new. (Why, for instance, is salsa not in a tube? Why, for instance, can we not make our own salsa fresh in the grocery store?) We flew through questions six and seven, then eight and nine, the Focus Group experimenting with the relationship of their respective bodies to the room, getting up from the table and walking around, some members leaning up against the room's walls, some lying down on the plush, cobalt carpet. This reapportioning, in turn, forced the FG Participants to push each other toward new processes and methods, and soon one FGP had taped his Stetson hat to a wall, and soon another had opened up her bag and pretended that it was a bowl of chips at a party. A makeup compact was turned into a salsa jar that was also a jet, the condiment made into flying machine and sent through the aisles of our ad hoc supermarket, a new sudden collage of military–industrial might, cylindrical glass, and rehydrated, imagined tomatoes. Questions ten and eleven were asked and answered, then twelve and thirteen, then fourteen and fifteen and so on, the Participants—evolved now, and believing in their own evolution, and having found individuality in heretofore unheard-of ways (one FG Member turning all his answers to a series of squawks and clucks that the rest of the Group then interpreted)—run through with an industriousness previously unmatched both by themselves and in comparison to any other Focus Group I had ever conducted. But this mechanization had a dark side, Gloria, too, as what was gained in the way of intellectual response and overall efficiency had the countereffect of detachment and isolation, each member now more important than the idea of the Group, until Zone 5 had broken itself up into schools, cliques, and factions. That is, Gloria, if we were once again unified in what the problem was, we had grown all the more divided in regard to how to solve it.

This sectioning off of thought and response also negated any real concern toward the continuing appearances of strangers in costumed garb specific to the region, even while these arrivals loudly deciphered The Stardust Room's half-locked doors, the lights flickering on and off whenever one of these strangers entered. Through the arrival of a rider for The Pony Express, then a pair of scantily clad burlesque dancers, then a miner, a Jesse James looka-like, a coolie, and finally, Gloria, a grizzled prospector with dented tin pan leading a donkey by a length of gnarled, frayed rope, the FG remained so entrenched in their various methods that the high-eared jack or jenny [I did not know its sex] made absolutely no impact on the group whatsoever, save for when the prospector asked aloud—as every single other entrant into The Stardust Room also had—Is This Rancho Brava? The Group bellowed in unison It Is Not, before returning, machinelike, to the questions at hand, Zone 5's answers to the questions I posed now arriving as a series of draw-ings, manifestos, and poems.

Lingering in my mind through this Focus Group "era" were thoughts of my ex-wife and our shared experiences: our early courtship through a hot summer in DC and the noise in the Georgetown bars that we went to; our first apartment, after we were engaged, and the shade of pale mint that we painted our bedroom; our by-bus commute from Wisconsin Ave. to Capitol Hill, where my wife, who temped for a lobbying firm, was told week after week of the beauty that her hands possessed, while she answered phones and passed files over the lip of her receptionist's desk and typed out responses to numerous emails; and then our decision to leave the East Coast after I was offered a position at the Los Angeles firm that I have since departed, the two of us renting a small cottage in Marina Del Rey before buying our now former home in Brentwood. It was at some point shortly after the closing of this house that a talent guy at a premiere West Coast "parts modeling" agency approached my wife in the Skin Products aisle of an organic grocery, telling the woman I loved how serendipitous it was to have located the talent innate in her limbs amongst the products that she would so soon be selling. Eighteen months later, my wife had been in almost two hundred ads, her hands framing sleek bottles of expensive perfume, her ring finger a backdrop for glittering, diamonded bands that cost as much as a Mercedes. She sold couscous, facial cream, keyboards, and iPods. She sold scarves and fly reels and purses. It was my wife's hands that appeared in *Vogue*, *Elle*, and *YM*. It was my wife's hands that "stood in" for numerous celebrities, the woman I married providing, in print ads, surrogate limbs for the likes of Cate Blanchett. It was my wife's hands that one saw on Vegas billboards, fingers fanned like beams of white sun over the toned, tanned stomach of a dancer for an all-male revue, her pinkies perhaps one inch away from the snap on this man's skin-tight black trousers. And it was my wife's hands that touched much more than that on other men, her palms placed on strangers' cheeks before sliding downward in secret, in silence.

After indisputable video evidence had been produced (I had hired a person to install, in the bedroom that I shared with my wife, a trio of hidden cameras, a decision that I still wrestle with today, despite the acts that these cameras caught on tape), and for some time after our divorce, I kept in a pocketed folder that I carried with me at nearly all times my wife's oeuvre, tearing out pages from those magazines in which my ex-wife had sold some certain product, in addition to creating video stills of the modeling spots that she did on television, and printing out these stills on high-quality photo paper to add to the folder. In a moment of utter misery and gloom that arrived out of nowhere roughly one month after all the papers had been signed and the house had been sold, and I was trying without much success to repair all parts of myself, I spread out these ads and stills on the clean, tan carpet of the Extended Stay suite in which I had been residing, staring at the collage I'd produced in the attempt, I believe, at attaching to it something approaching prescience—that amongst all these images of my wife's hands, I might be able to locate foreknowledge of her terrible, adulterous happenings. But prescience after the fact serves no one at all, even if one is able to locate it, and later that night, after two scotches in the lobby's small bar, I repaired the collection of paper to the dumpster behind the hotel, lifting the heavy, ridged top of the bin with one hand and tossing my wife's ads (and by extension, a portion of myself) into its wide and dark belly.

The alley was well lit by sodium lights that glowed a white-blue and were attached to the wall of the building, and it was late, Gloria, late enough that even sections of the Los Angeles basin were quiet, and after I set the lid of the dumpster back down, the plastic barely making a sound as it met with the metal, I looked down the alley, toward the front of the hotel. The smooth asphalt, light gray and unspoiled by droplets of oil or burnished by the rubber of car tires, matched exactly the color of the alley's high walls, which in turned matched the color of the underlit clouds that had pushed in from the ocean, the whole world, it seemed, resetting to one single hue, the natural and manmade in that moment merging, history lost in the fog of greater LA or buried under new, antiseptic construction. It lent the idea—and perhaps the feeling, too—that anything at all was possible, the choices unlimited and nearly brand new, and of diminishing worth, and spawning only more choices, which in turned spawned more, until it was impossible for anyone to remember what the original choice was, or how it might have ever mattered. Five minutes later, I went back up to my room. The next morning, I received the call from my firm about conducting a Focus Group in West Texas.

Zone 5 finished the packet with ease, returning to the conference table and assembling their things as we prepared our farewells and found our cell phones and car keys. In those moments, though, as a long round of pleasantries was fizzling out like the last batch of fireworks at a July display, our Focus Group received its final visitor, the individual arriving quietly enough that none in Zone 5 initially noticed. This person's entrance was lost upon, me, too, as (1) I was turned away from the door due to ejecting the DVD from its player, my body at perhaps a 140 degree angle in relation to the front of room and my peripheral vision all but useless, and (2) for the first and only time during the FG, the lights on the wagon wheel nearest the door didn't flicker as the banquet room's threshold was crossed. As I had come to rely on this visual cue for the day's many person-based interruptions, I continued my conversation with that Focus Group member who held the most outspoken belief in the Christian God, the two of us discussing an area café that produced an excellent cheeseburger. 'Merican food, the woman said, and then a second Focus Group member tapped me on the shoulder.

While in the parking lot, later, the police would call our last entrant by his proper name, for purposes of this letter, Gloria, and, in an attempt at concealing his identity, I will refer to the man in question as the Very Inebriated Native American, or VINA—nomenclature justified by the Lubbock PD's on-site Blood Alcohol Reading, the VINA blowing into the hard plastic straw to reveal that he was more than three times over the legal limit. This fact was one that was impossible to know upon the VINA's arrival, however, as there was nothing contained in the man's posture or gait that might have allowed myself or anyone else to infer that the VINA was just that—highly intoxicated. Indeed, as I turned my head to respond to the tap on the shoulder and looked past the Focus Group Participant offering the tap, to the man in question, the first thing that raised a proverbial red flag was that, unlike the other strangers' costumes or ware, the VINA's outfit seemed only partial. While he had on a headdress and moccasin shoes, he was also in cut-off denim shorts and a loose gray tank-top t-shirt, on the front of which was written, in neon curling font, SEE THE GRAND CANYON. The words ran diagonally, from the southwest corner of the fabric all the way to the northeast, just above and to the right of the VINA's left nipple.

May I Help You, I said to the man, fully expecting him to answer my question with a question, specifically, Is This Rancho Brava? When no verbal response was offered at all, I asked the question again, as many of the FGPs were still talking amongst themselves, and I was a sizable distance (ten yards? fifteen?) from the VINA. However, when I received no reply from the man for a second time, I admit that I began scrutinize him. A number of aesthetic details stood out: the rattiness of the VINA's denim shorts, the stains (beef broth? dried blood?) near the bottom hem of the man's tank top, the tomahawk tattoo across the man's left shin, and the small leather scabbard clipped to a belt loop of the VINA's cutoffs, some feet above the tattoo of the tomahawk. From afar, the hunting knife's blade looked at least an inch wide, and the light from the wagon wheel fixture overhead glinted off the visible portion of the blade (just above the hilt) in a way where I was absolutely sure the weapon was metal. The headdress's plumes—naturally white, with sections of them dyed red and black—swung up and curved back from the man's forehead, a single feather dangling from each side of the cap at the temples, trailing over the VINA's exposed, narrow shoulders.

And while the juxtaposition, Gloria, of the VINA's culture-specific garb and more status quo clothing choices, along with the knife, the tattoo, and the ongoing lack of anything approaching verbal recognition of my twice-asked question, were all causing in me very real concern, I remained unsure of whether or not there was a need to take action, my indecision extending out of a trio of ideas counter to the notion that the VINA was unwell and/or dangerous. The first of these ideas can be titled Clothing Trends, an aspect of society, Gloria, about which I know little, especially in regard to what may or may not be à la mode in any given year or season. That is, it seemed possible to me that some if not all components of the VINA's outfit were self-aware or even postmodern choices, ones that championed above all else ironic detachment. In the same way that some youthful portions of contemporary America wear clothes from a different decade (I am thinking here, Gloria, of 60s wide-bottomed jeans, or 70s leather jackets), it seemed well within the realm of possibility that the headdress, the moccasins, and perhaps even the knife were having their original purpose or place in the spectrum of fashion be reimagined, if not reconstructed, and the VINA's ethnic background was purely coincidental, as opposed to being the driving force behind his clothing choices; that is, even if there is a certain sardonic aspect to a Native American hipster sporting a headdress and moccasins, cynical derision is common in youth, and the VINA himself, only twenty-two, certainly fit into such a post-teen, angst-ridden demographic (one I might add, Gloria, that has the potential to feel most consistently the need to "fit in" by making all manner of social choice its members might not otherwise make, were it not for the need to norm themselves by rebelling in prescribed and established ways, ones that often linger only through youth and remain at a literal and/or figurative surface level).

The second idea that kept me from action ran converse to the thinking supporting Clothing Trends and can be titled Sociocultural Differences. That is, if the "Clothing Trends" theory dealt largely with the obliteration of a substantive interpretation of the real, the "Sociocultural Differences" idea upheld it, the validity of such a posit grounded in the stark reality of day-to-day to life for the majority of Native Americans: that they (Native Americans, or American Indians, Gloria, if you prefer) live in abject poverty on some of the blankest, barest lands America has to offer; that their communities are riddled with alcohol, drug, and physical abuse; that these communities harbor the highest rates of suicide and mental disorders of any communities on the continent of North America; that the startling dearth of employment opportunities only exacerbates the aforementioned truths; and that they (Native Americans/American Indians) arrive at this collective societal malaise due to their deceitful and abhorrent treatment at the hands of the American Anglo's westward expansion. That is, Gloria, when I stared at the VINA, I stared also at my own doings, as my ancestors arrived on the East Coast from Europe, and these ancestors did at the very least accept if not participate in the massacring of Native American populations, after which, from what I was told by my own parents (now deceased), these ancestors went South, where they owned a cotton plantation, which meant the people who eventually, and by extension, spawned me, also enslaved African Americans.

But I'm getting away from my point, Gloria. Guilt can do that. Guilt can fracture the light of truth the way funhouse mirrors can bend one's reflection. It was like that for me, poring through hours of digital video of my wife's dalliances, a lamb at the altar of grief, sure that my union's shortcomings were my own my fault, and not my spouse's. Here's what I mean: the VINA was no hipster at all, and the costume, while partial, was the best he could manage, a fact that seemed justifiable, given the startling disenfranchisement the VINA had almost certainly endured for the whole of his short existence, a life of constraints that defied mitigation, one governed most often by madness and doom, and whose only certain trait was uncertainty. That is, the VINA was bringing to the table the very best that he could, given his subjective, adverse circumstances. To bring to light his costume's deficiencies (and assuming indeed that his vestments were costume) would reveal me as just another unsympathetic white man of the kind that the VINA and his family before him had endured, Gloria, for centuries.

The last idea that kept me from taking action of any sort was Rancho Brava. Even as the VINA's actions began to escalate, the young man now approaching Focus Group Participants individually, breaching each FGP's personal space and getting so close to them that the two parties were almost touching noses, I still wasn't sure, Gloria, that this wasn't part of an act that perhaps served as warm-up for that other banquet room's almost certainly spirited happenings. Tied into this was the VINA saying aloud the phrase from his shirt to each FG Participant he approached. See The Grand Canyon, the VINA would say, and one of the Zone 5 FGPs would counter with, Get Away From Me, or You Smell Like A Booze Factory. When the VINA received a response, he would move on, repeating the phrase—See The Grand Canyon—from person to person to person, each FG Participant startled and confused, until the VINA approached the FG with that strongest proclivity to the Christian God and removed his knife from its scabbard.

It would be unfair, though, Gloria, to say that even this brandishing of a weapon was enough to cause true alarm, as the VINA was by no means the first stranger of southwestern personage to arrive to The Stardust Room armed. Davey Crockett had stood a musket up by the door, and one of the members of Mariachi Errante had a small can of mace attached to his keychain. Furthermore, the sheriff had twin holstered guns, as did both the Pony Express rider and the Jesse James lookalike. Abstracted, one could also contend that the prospector had a weapon in the form of his burro. (I was surprised, Gloria, that the Marriott chain of hotels allowed pack animals on its premises, regardless of the events in its banquet rooms. Such animals, especially in confined quarters, become highly unpredictable, and the possibility for injury from trampling or a bite would seem to increase almost exponentially, as would the possibility for litigation on the part of any person injured by an incensed, panicked donkey.) That is, Gloria, the FG Participants, much like myself, were struggling with understanding the VINA's true intentions, as the VINA's context could not be concretely defined, given that the reasons for the VINA's repeated phrase and brandishing of his short knife were mutable: was the VINA making fun of our assumed perception of him, and was that perception, Gloria, true? Or, alternately, did the FG Participants and myself want so badly to have our assumed perception not be true that we were ignoring very obvious warning signals? Or, thirdly, did the VINA believe, as others had, that he might actually be in Rancho Brava at present and had simply begun an act that made sense there but not here, in the confines of The Stardust Room, where we'd explored salsa?

These variables bounced up and disappeared at a rate similar to those plastic creatures comprising a Whack-a-Mole game common to many family fun establishments, and I found myself, Gloria—even as the VINA pulled out his knife, took the Very Christian FGP by the back of her hair, and said, It Is Now My Duty to Scalp You—so overwhelmed by the rapidity of choice that I could only stand there, figurative mallet in hand, and do nothing. In hindsight, I believe my inertia to have been caused by the notion that the entities seeking out Rancho Brava were all individuals representative of regional clichés, those parts of society that through their very nature cannot evolve or progress in the slightest. That is, Gloria, it seemed somehow impossible to me that an entity as antiquated and provincial as a "drunk Indian" might actually be able to assert itself on 21st century, globalized culture (i.e., myself and the Zone 5 FGPs). Have we not, as a society, transcended role-based, regional expressions because they have lost all ingenuity? And if so, Gloria, then why do they remain? Why is it that one *does* go and see the Grand Canyon?

The Very Christian FGP, her eyes now wide with horror, the top half of her body pulled back over her hips as though she were balancing precariously on the lip of a cliff and trying desperately not to fall off of it, stared at the VINA as the man raised his knife, her arms flapping wildly, the oversized silver cross at the vertex of her necklace emerging from under the chest of her blouse and swinging back and forth ever so slightly. The VINA, meanwhile, who up to this point had maintained a visage of utter calm, so much so that he looked virtually bored by what he was doing, turned his head to the ceiling of The Stardust Room and held the knife up even higher, gaining more leverage before his ostensible plunging down of the weapon. These dual actions forced a range of small sounds from the other Focus Group Participants, the most common being a sort of breathless, visceral *oh*, as though those FGPs making the sound had touched a hand to something unexpectedly hot and wounded themselves in the process. (Other responses included No, Stop, Holy Shit, and Oh Fuck, though as stated these were outnumbered by the ohs, which arrived en masse and as a sort of unintended chorus.)

At that moment, Gloria, all concern vanished from my mind, as I prepared to witness a human death for the very first time. I forgot about my ex-wife, our turmoil and joy. I forgot about salsa and the Focus Group Packets. I forgot my profession, my name, and my sex. I existed only as matter that emitted no light, about to expand and become my horizon. What stopped this from occurring was a former All Big-12 Oklahoma State University linebacker. Darby "Bull" Dozer, born nearby, in New Deal, TX, was a four-year starter for his alma mater Cowboys, a fact that he mentioned at the Focus Group's outset and that returned to me as he blindsided the VINA, tackling the very drunk young man to the carpeted floor with such force that the would-be assailant was forced to let go of his weapon, the knife twirling as it dropped, landing inches from the left tennis shoe of the woman who was to receive the scalping. The former linebacker wrestled in high school, too, and choked out the VINA with a "sleeper hold" in a matter of seconds, the other FG Participants issuing cheers that Dozer would have been proud to receive during his varsity days in Stillwater.

And that, Gloria, was largely that—the police were called, the VINA taken in, the Focus Group Participants and myself all departing The Stardust Room and preparing to return to our respective lives. There was no exchanging of phone numbers, Twitter handles, email addresses, or Facebook account information. Some of us followed the police as they took the VINA outside, where we watched the Lubbock PD issue a Breathalyzer Test then guide the VINA's body into the back of the squad car. The hotel manager issued a public apology at the end of this scene, saying how sorry he was that we were forced to endure such acts of intimidation and violence on hotel grounds and offering up coupons for a free night's stay at any Marriot hotel in the continental United States, before walking stiffly and quickly back through the tinted, automatic front doors of the establishment. I stood in the parking lot, the sun hot on my face, the wind carrying on it the soft, rich scent of smoke from a distant wildfire. Some FGPs waved at me as they drove off in their pickups, minivans or compacts. I followed the hotel manager back inside, re-entering The Stardust Room, Gloria, but only barely, as a foot ahead of me, on the cobalt-colored carpet, was the wagon wheel chandelier that had been blinking on and off for the full of the day—its chain had snapped, and the fixture was now lying on the floor in three pieces.

I let the door shut behind me and walked around the wrecked wheel, staring at the smattering of glass from the cracked bulbs and the fixture's exposed, curling wiring. Up close, it was easy to tell that the wheel was indeed real wood and held chips and splinters from which one at least could infer that the item was part of a long journey west, away from the dense forests of Vermont or Virginia, trundling sturdily through the Midwest before traversing, somehow, the long seams of the Rockies, its trip likely ending somewhere after that, the wood pulled apart by the dry desert wind, the disc left to rot next to a creosote-tinged slab of fluorite. But it didn't rot, Gloria. It made it here, to the ceiling then the floor of The Stardust Room, the wheel important enough, in some manner or way, not to have been left to decay at the base of a bluff, near a den of sidewinders. Instead, it was adapted for a different sort of use, rethought and reused, exactly the same and yet very much different.

It wasn't until I had unplugged the TV and was wheeling the device on its rickety stand back toward the room's doors that I realized that the VINA had in all likelihood saved at least one Focus Group Member from death, even while attempting to take the life of another, as were it not for the VINA's entrée and his subsequent actions, it seems likely to me that one FGP would have been walking under the chandelier as it loosed and fell, maiming badly if not taking the life of that person. I stood there, palms on the TV stand as if I were pushing a cart and thought about what such a chain of events could mean—that the VINA's detainment equated to the preservation of life for a Focus Group Member—then gave up trying to ascertain a solution, returning the TV to the hotel's front desk, and that night eating at the establishment recommended by the Very Christian Focus Group Participant (the burger's meat, Gloria, was full of fat, and its flavors were far too aggressive.)

When I returned to the hotel, all of the parking spaces near the lobby doors were full. I guided my sedan around the side of a building, parking in a free space in front of a thin, gnarled cottonwood tree trapped in a floral version of coma: while not truly dead, it seemed less than alive, never again to produce new buds and instead spend the rest of its existence in some form of suspended animation. Yards away from the tree was one of the hotel's side entrances, and after two tries I was able to get my key card to work in its security system. Feet ahead of me, on the left side of the corridor, was the entrance to Rancho Brava. I looked down the hall, toward the front desk, and seeing no sign of human life, I walked toward the twin mahogany doors, lightly trying first one and then the other handle. Neither would depress. I set my shoulder bag down, looking back toward the front desk one more time. Turning my torso to one side, I pressed my left ear to the laminated wood, blinking my eyes as I tried to listen for any sounds coming from inside the room, any clue that might explain the day's actions. I stood there ten seconds, awkwardly crouched, the cartilage around my ear canal beginning to throb from pressure. I readjusted, then put a finger in my free ear, shutting my eyes and standing perfectly still and letting my body, as best as it could, give itself wholly over to the act of aural surveillance. At one point, I thought that I heard a Yeeee-Whoooo, and, at a second, I thought that I could discern the clinking of glasses, two crystal vessels meeting with force, their collision a jubilant salute to the West's past and its cultures and customs. But I know that I did not hear these things—that the boomtown yawp and the sound of the glasses meeting in toast existed only in my imagination. As I drew back from the door, though, Gloria, the most impossible of things happened.

I had just grabbed the strap of my shoulder bag and was getting ready to walk toward the elevators when one and then both of Rancho Brava's door handles started jiggling, the chrome-finished levers flipping up and down a half-inch, and with startling rapidity. Someone was in there, Gloria, and trying to get out, the two handles making clicking sounds as a person or persons madly shook them. I backed away from the entrance, unsure of what to do, my heart beating faster and my mouth going wet as I looked down the Marriott's hall, toward the lobby. Again, however, no patron or employee could be seen, and as I was trying to make the decision of whether to call out, go for help, or simply just leave, the handles began to shake even faster on their circular mounts, until the two pieces of metal turned red and popped free from the doors, falling to the carpeted floor in front of me.

Amazed, my mind flipping through answers likes files in a drawer, I bent down and touched at one of the levers with a finger. It was still hot, and, as I drew my hand away, I looked toward the freshly made holes in the entrance to Rancho Brava, now being at eye level with them. If lights were on in the room, something or someone stood in the way of their illumination, as when I pressed my face to first the left hole, then the right, all that I saw was blackness, the sort of all-consuming blackness one can sometimes stand in,

Gloria, on lightless nights in the middle of the desert, the stars and the moon blocked out by clouds, the contours of the world having vanished.

I waited five minutes, my eye still pressed to the hole, moving back and forth to look through one and then the other, hoping that whatever barrier that stood in the way might remove itself but also not being so brave as to insert a digit and try to touch at the impediment, if such a blockade were indeed in place, as it seemed just as possible that the reason I couldn't view the interior of the room was that all of the lights in Rancho Brava were off in the first place. Either way, Gloria, enough time had passed where I had come back into possession of my self-awareness, cognizant of the fact that, while an act that I still can't explain had just occurred, I was also crouched in front of a hotel banquet room door like a criminal or idiot. I stood to leave, swinging my shoulder bag's strap over my body, then noticing my shoe was untied, and just as I was about to bend back down and tie it, an item was loosed through the space of the door, falling to the floor inches in front of me.

Gloria, today I turned thirty-nine. The second act of my play is one year away, and even now the house lights have begun their dimming. I have no spouse, no children, no mortgage. I do not own a pet and harbor no debt. I've donated my loafers and dress shirts and neckties. The ghosts of my past inhabit faraway lands and, while some mean me harm, they won't ever find me. If this next decade, for most, is one of profession and family, and the settling in for the trip down that (perhaps pleasant) road of subscribing and ascribing, I find myself on a different sort of path, one largely unpaved and set back from Life's highway, the dust my tires bring up something near to a shield, the miles ahead of me absent of traffic. Another way, perhaps, of saying this, Gloria, is that while I never saw who was in Rancho Brava that day, I know that person's identity, because I was in Rancho Brava. A version of me shook the room's door handles to hot, and once those implements fell to the floor, I was given a gift that only I could give me. What this item is doesn't matter at all. Its worth lies only in its continued importance.

Shady Lanes Trailer Court is managed by Ken Nakahara, a Vietnam Vet and retired park ranger. I'm in his doublewide now, my laptop attached by a cord to his printer. Once this letter's done, we'll sit in Shady Lane's "park," a two-plot swath of lawn abutting Ken's home that harbors good shade from a trio of mesquites, under which is a single wood picnic table. Ken's worked in Black Canyon and Capitol Reef and spent his last years at Red Rock, in Nevada. His knowledge is vast, and his ministrations of it tactical and humble. In my acceptance of him as a steward of the land, he has found in me his final student. We sit often at sundown, drinking iced instant coffee, Ken recounting his years in the forest and deserts. We'll never travel together—this seems understood. Instead, his wisdom is a baton handed off, my neighbor's length of the race having come to an end as my portion of the relay is beginning. Tomorrow, I may drive southwest, toward Juarez. Tomorrow, I may take I-40 and then 25 toward Trinidad, CO. If neither of these, I will wind up somewhere in between: Albuquerque or Flagstaff or Durango. In the meantime, I've not checked my email for months. I have only a vague notion of my checking account balance. I own one pair of footwear—my hiking boots. They've not even begun to truly break in. They will last for me decades. They may outlast me.

Gloria, I hope that this letter helps you, and that all is well in Milford, CT. I imagine come fall that the trees will turn red. I imagine, next to them, a Protestant church's bone white spire, slimming as it ascends toward thick, moody clouds whose voyage will shortly become transatlantic. I don't think that I'll see the East Coast again. A boundary was lowered and I chose to step past it, and now that I have, there's no want to go back. Instead, I rocket outward over alien lands. Instead, I search for chuckwalla basking on dolostone slabs, in the pulsing dusk light of my low, endless desert.

Books in the Series

21st Century Prose
Series editor: Matthew Vollmer, Virginia Tech

The 21st Century Prose series celebrates varieties of forms—of prose that breaks the rules, bends conventions, and reconfigures genre. The books in this series engage playfulness and experimentation without sacrificing accessibility and readability. The voices represented in the series come alive on the page through prose that is at once down-to-earth and also a reflection of an artist at home with his or her improvisations. Life-affirming but convention-defying, the language in these books strives to be both groundbreaking and readable. The 21st Century Prose series listens for and endorses voices that have been marginalized, reports from zones—physical and spiritual and emotional—from which we have yet to hear. Kind-hearted renegades. Things we can't describe but that leave us pleasantly puzzled, forcing us to say, "listen, just read it."

Books in the Series:

Printed and bound by CPI Group (UK) Ltd, Croydon, CR0 4YY

13/04/2025

14656529-0004